"We've been waiting for you, Puma . . ."

said a voice from the darkness.

I turned, and two figures came toward me. They were men—short and heavy set, but I couldn't see their faces clearly.

"Business?" I asked casually.

"Yeah," said one of them. "One grand just to keep your nose out of the Ryerson kill. It's worth a grand to us."

I shook my head. "The cops will think it mighty strange if I pull out now."

"You don't have to make any announcements. A smart private eye like you should know how to goof off."

"I must be getting close to the killer," I said quietly, "or you boys wouldn't be worried. Sorry. No dice."

The one on the right came first, crowding me against my car. I felt the door handle in my back, and he hooked a left into my belly.

I lifted a knee and heard him grunt. Then I found his throat and started to tear out his Adam's apple.

He gurgled out a choked scream—as the other one sapped me from the side.

"Goddam snooping shamus," he muttered.

Redness flooded my brain as I went down.

END OF A Call Girl

William Campbell Gault

Adams Media
New York London Toronto Sydney New Delhi

Adams Media
An Imprint of Simon & Schuster, Inc.
57 Littlefield Street
Avon, Massachusetts 02322

For information about special discounts for bulk purchases, please contact Simon & Schuster Special Sales at 1-866-506-1949 or business@simonandschuster.com.

Manufactured in the United States of America

Library of Congress Cataloging-in-Publication Data has been applied for.

ISBN 978-1-4405-5793-4
ISBN 978-1-4405-3914-5 (ebook)

This work has been previously published in print format by: Fawcett World Library, New York, NY.

For

THE FICTIONEERS

ONE

SHE WAS all of forty, but remarkably well-preserved, a shapely imitation blonde with an artfully made-up face, wearing a mink stole and an expensively tailored suit.

She sat in my office peevishly explaining the perils of her trade. Her trade was call girls, the hundred-dollar-and-up kind. She was no longer personally active but ran a list and would occasionally fill a date if the mood was on her and the customer tolerant. At least, that's what she told me.

"The studio trade isn't what it used to be," she said sadly, "but we get a lot of visiting Texans. They can be rough on the girls, though, those Texans."

I leaned back in my chair, doodling on a pad, and wondered why she was telling me all this. She was finishing a joke about a Texan with a big belt buckle when I asked her.

I asked, "Why are you telling me all this?"

She stopped talking to frown at me. Finally, "I wanted to be honest with you. Frank told me that was the way to be."

"Frank—? Frank who?"

"Frank Perini. Didn't I tell you he had recommended you to me?"

"No, you didn't, Mrs. Diggert. Did he also tell you I work only within the law?"

She shook her head, her gaze slightly belligerent.

"He should have," I said. "And your—business is outside the law, isn't it?"

She shook her head again. "My girls are listed as models and entertainers. You could say I run a—lonely hearts service."

"An ultimate service," I added.

Her voice was sharp. "Frank's outside the law. Frank's a gambler. And you worked for him."

"What I did for Frank Perini had nothing to do with his trade. I merely found his son for him."

"So? And all I want you to do for me is find a friend of mine."

"That's different," I agreed. "Who is the friend?"

"A girl named Jean Talsman. She was to meet a man at the Beverly Canyon Motel yesterday. She never kept the appointment and I haven't been able to get in touch with her since."

I asked quietly. "A friend? Or one of your girls, Mrs. Diggert?"

"As far as you need be concerned, Mr. Puma, the girl is simply a friend."

"In that case, couldn't you go to the police with your story?"

She glared at me, saying nothing.

"I hope that doesn't sound too moral," I apologised. "I'm not exactly Galahad, but I do have to stay in business and that means I must be careful. Now, tell me honestly, why didn't you go to the police?"

"Because," Mrs. Diggert said, "the man she was supposed to meet is a married man. Now, trot out your morality, Mr. Puma. Is there anything moral about ruining the respectable name of a husband and father?"

"It was a risk the man himself was taking."

"So? That was *his* morality he was risking. Ruining his name would be on *my* conscience."

I smiled and said nothing.

"And I'll make it clearer, as long as we're on the subject. My girls get from a hundred dollars a night—an evening, up. They are permitted to—choose their company. They could have landed in a less respectable end of this ancient profession where they sold a piece of their souls ten times a night at three dollars a piece. My girls promise nobody anything."

I still said nothing.

"I could have gone to a dozen other investigators in this town who aren't concerned with ethics."

"You didn't. You still can."

"I don't want to. Listen, Puma, how many commandments are there?"

"Ten."

"Then why," she asked, "when a woman is called an 'immoral woman' does it mean only one of the commandments has been violated. Nobody ever imagines it could be one of the other nine."

"We have a Puritan tradition in this country," I explained.

"Who actually lives it?"

I doodled some more.

"Say no if you're going to, Mr. Puma. I won't beg any more."

"I get a hundred a day and expenses," I explained.

She chuckled. "My girls don't get expenses." She lifted a huge black purse from her lap. "Are you accepting my business?"

I nodded. "And all you are really concerned with is finding the girl? That's the unvarnished truth?"

She stared. "What else?"

"I'm not supposed to drag her back, or anything?"

She sighed wearily. "What in hell do you think I am? They're free to quit me any time they want to. I'm not their keeper; I'm their—well, agent would be the word, I guess. Jean, Mr. Puma, is a very close personal friend of mine."

From the black purse she took out a four by five portrait of Jean Talsman which she handed me. I took down the rest of the pertinent information. Her home address was in Brentwood; her age was twenty-six; her linage was 36-22-38.

Mrs. Dora Diggert said, "Two days should do it, don't you think?" She put a pair of hundred dollar bills on my desk. "You can bill me for the expenses later."

"And your address?" I asked.

"The phone number is all you'll need," she told me. "It's an unlisted number. And here is all I know about the date Jean was supposed to have had." She handed me a page of single-spaced information.

Then she stood up. She stood well, shoulders back and chin high. There is something that gets me about attractive and successful women in any line; I admired her as she stood there.

She smiled, studying me. "I'm not that attractive."

"Success always impresses me," I explained. "I must have a lot of Rotary in me."

She continued to smile. "Well, if you ever get a hundred or two you don't know what to do with—" She looked at the bills still on the desk.

"I'm a poor man, Mrs. Diggert," I said sadly. "I can only afford the amateurs."

She left and I sat there, studying the picture of Jean Talsman. It was a highly attractive face, sensitive, faintly defiant. If I were a girl, I wondered, would I sell out? If I were a girl, I would be a two hundred and nine pound girl and it was doubtful if I would find a buyer even if I did make the ultimate surrender.

It was now noon; I had lunch before driving over to the office of George Ryerson. Mr. Ryerson was a C.P.A. and had his own small but busy firm of accountants. It seemed unlikely that an accountant named George could be responsible for Miss Talsman's disappearance, but it seemed more unlikely that he would have phoned for a call girl in the first place. And he had.

The office was on Wilshire, on the second floor of a new building in a good district. The waiting room was conservatively and tastefully furnished and the red-headed receptionist a perfect example of brick-house Irish. This George was doing all right.

The redhead wanted me to state my business. I told her it was personal.

"Does Mr. Ryerson know you by name?"

I shook my head. "Nor by sight. Just run in and tell him Mrs. Diggert sent me."

She frowned. "Mrs. Diggert—? I'm not familiar with that name."

"I'm glad. But maybe Mr. Ryerson is? Why don't you trot in and ask him?"

She picked up the phone on her desk, threw a key, and said, "Mr. Ryerson, a Mr. Puma is here, sent here by a

Mrs. Diggert. I have no record of any appointment for him."

Silence for a second and then, "Yes, sir, I'll send him right in."

She looked at me blandly and explained it was the office at the end of the hall and went back to her own concerns.

The office at the end of the hall was the big one, naturally, and George had furnished it in masculine leather and masculine Bellows prints and a masculine portable bar. I would think a man in his business would get some female trade out here but the room didn't look like he expected any.

He was a tall, faintly beefy man with thinning hair and excellent tailoring. He got up to shake my hand and seat me and then went back to sit behind his desk.

From there, he asked, "How can I help you, Mr. Puma?"

"By telling me what happened to Jean Talsman."

He frowned. "Jean—Talsman—? Is she one of Dora's girls?"

"She's the one you ordered," I said, "two nights ago."

He shook his head empathically. "I asked for no girl by name. Has something happened to Miss Talsman?"

"Mrs. Diggert specifically stated that you asked for Jean by name. And asked her to come to the Beverly Canyon Motel. Didn't you tell Mrs. Diggert that the girl didn't show up?"

He nodded. "I told her that, yes. But I didn't mention any name."

"According to Mrs. Diggert, you never asked for Jean Talsman or any other girl before. Where did you learn about her?"

"Mr. Puma," he said patiently, "I don't like to contradict Mrs. Diggert, but I didn't ask for any Jean Talsman. I said I'd take any girl." He was blushing now.

"How long did you wait for her?" I asked.

He said stiffly, "I fail to see how that's important."

I said, "The girl is missing. Let me decide what's important."

His voice was cold. "Don't be insolent, Mr. Puma. You're not the police, you know. You have no official position."

"Right," I agreed. "Perhaps it would be better if we went to the police with this."

He looked at his desk top. "That wouldn't do Mrs. Diggert's business any good, would it?"

"It would hurt it less than it would hurt yours," I pointed out. "Dora's clientele aren't real fussy about her reputation, but I'm sure your clients might be disturbed."

He said nothing.

"Also," I went on, "Dora's divorced. You're not, are you, Mr. Ryerson?"

He glared at me. "Are you threatening me with disclosure?"

"Not exactly. I'm simply trying to get some cooperation out of you."

"I have told Mrs. Diggert all I know."

"You mean you answered some questions she asked. She had to phone you to ask them, didn't she? You never complained that the girl hadn't shown up, not until Mrs. Diggert phoned. Why not?"

"Because it wasn't important."

"You're a businessman, Mr. Ryerson. Do you mean to say you don't put in a complaint when a supplier fails to deliver?"

He expelled his breath and looked at me acidly. "You're being absurd. This was after business hours. This had nothing to do with business."

I threw out a random shot on a hunch. "Perhaps you weren't even waiting at the motel. Perhaps you ordered the girl for one of your clients?"

His gaze was blank. "Perhaps."

"Who was the client?"

"I said 'perhaps.' Mr. Puma, I've told you and Mrs. Diggert all I know. You'll have to decide what to do with it."

I said honestly, "It's not our decision to make. If we feel that she is actually missing and not of her own free will, we will automatically have to go to the police." I stood up. "That is no threat, believe me. I don't and can't exist in opposition to the Police Department."

He said doubtfully, "Dora Diggert will never go running to the police. It would ruin her."

"I doubt it. But it would ruin me if I were given a missing persons case and did not notify them of it eventually. If you want to ruin me, Mr. Ryerson, phone them and tell them what I just asked you."

He stood up. "Sorry I couldn't be of more help, Mr. Puma. Good day."

"Good afternoon," I said. "I hope I don't have to come back."

I went back down the hall and past the redhead in the reception room and out to my car. My next stop would be the motel, but I wasn't thinking of that.

I was thinking that George Ryerson had made quite an issue of an apparently unimportant incident. What importance could there be in the fact that he had asked for a specific girl? Why had he denied it?

This was the first time he had used the services of Dora Diggert; so it was logical to assume he knew Jean through some other social medium. Had he met her recently or known her for a longer length of time?

Of course there was always the possibility that he was telling the truth and Mrs. Diggert was lying. One fact seemed certain; one of them was lying. A lie must have a reason and reasons are often revealing.

A third thought came to me. Perhaps George didn't know Jean Talsman but his client did and George had ordered her by name for the client. Which could indicate that the girl wouldn't have gone if she had known who the true customer was.

In these days of saturation taxation, C.P.A.'s get a variety of accounts and not all of them are socially respectable. The Internal Revenue boys had picked up too many hoodlums that the F.B.I. had failed on. It was smart for racketeers these days to hire the best accounting brains they could find.

But this was all speculation. Facts were my business.

At the Beverly Canyon Motel, I found the manager in his office. It was a luxury motel with an eighty foot pool, with a putting green and a first-rate restaurant attached. It was logical to expect that the manager of such a snooty spot would not be unduly cooperative with anything as plebian as a private investigator.

He lived up to the pattern. He wouldn't even tell me if a George Reimers had rented a unit two evenings back. That was the name Ryerson was supposed to have used at the motel.

I said, "A woman who was supposed to have come here to meet Mr. Reimers is missing, sir. We're not looking for scandal, only a missing woman."

His eyebrows rose. "Scandal? Who mentioned scandal?"

"I did. The word shouldn't be unfamiliar to a motel manager."

He stared at me thoughtfully.

I said, "I'm here in lieu of the police. If I don't find this girl, rest assured that the police will be your next visitors. I repeat, I'm not looking for trouble."

He continued to stare at me for a few seconds. Then he picked up the phone on his desk. He asked for the clerk and told him, "A Mr. Puma would like to check our guest cards for night before last. He is on the way there now."

He didn't say any more to me, not even good-bye.

The desk clerk was an elderly man in a conservative suit but sporting a spectacular tie and a slight odor of lavender. He had the registration cards ready for me when I arrived at the desk.

George Reimers has been assigned to number 22-A. His signature didn't look like the careful writing one would expect from a C.P.A.

I asked the clerk, "Do you remember the man?"

He nodded. "Fairly short man, but stocky."

That description didn't fit George Ryerson. I asked, "Thinning hair?"

"Oh, no. A full head of black hair."

"Are you sure? How about his tailoring?"

"I'm sure. His tailoring was . . . well, I suppose it could be called expensive. But . . . rather, oh . . . George Raftish, if you know what I mean."

"Did he have any visitors?"

He nodded immediately. "Ah, yes. A beautiful girl. They sat in the patio, of course. We don't have visitors in the rooms unless—"

I interrupted him by taking out the picture of Jean Talsman. "Would you recognize the girl?" I put the portrait on the desk.

He held it up and looked at it for a few seconds. Then he said quietly, "That's the girl. I'm certain of it."

"How long did she stay?"

The clerk frowned. "I don't remember when she left.

Nor he. He didn't have any luggage, so he paid in advance and we have no record of his check-out time."

"Was there anything else about them you noticed?"

He looked at me skeptically. "Noticed . . . ?"

"You remember them both so well I thought you might have given them a little—extra interest."

"I remember a great number of our guests. But I don't pry, Mr. Puma."

"Nothing more you can tell me, then?"

"Nothing," he said primly.

I thanked him and went into the bar off the lobby. I ordered a bottle of Eastern beer and put together what I had learned. Ryerson had lied. He'd lied twice.

He was not the man Jean Talsman was supposed to meet here, but the girl had come here to meet a man, a man registered under the name Ryerson was supposed to have used.

This could have happened: Ryerson arranged the meeting for one of his clients at the client's request. The client had known Jean Talsman, but preferred to use a different name, for some reason. Jean had come here and met the man. And gone off with him? That I didn't know.

But when Dora phoned Ryerson, he was on a spot. He didn't know what had happened at the motel, so had tried to divorce himself from any involvement by claiming the girl had not fulfilled the date. For some reason, he couldn't reveal the name of his client, and this flimsy lie had been his first response.

I phoned him from a booth in the bar.

The girl who answered the phone told me he had just left for lunch and she didn't know when he would be back. I left my name.

I phoned Dora at her unlisted number and told her, "I'm at a temporary dead end." I told her what I had learned.

"That miserable Ryerson," she fumed. "I didn't think he'd know what to do with a girl. I should have been suspicious when he phoned for one."

"How did he happen to have your number, Dora?"

"He's done some work for me, income tax work."

"How about Jean's friends?" I asked. "Is there any girl she's particularly close to?"

"The girl she lives with. The address is on that paper I

gave you. She and I aren't friends so I don't know whether she lied to me or not when I phoned about Jean."

"Is this girl home during the day?"

"Some days. She's a model. Aren't you going back to ask Ryerson why he lied?"

"He just left for lunch. I'll get back at him as soon as possible. I don't want to waste any time waiting."

"Good boy, Puma. And keep my name out of it."

I didn't promise that. I could try to, but I couldn't promise I'd be successful. I climbed into the Plymouth and drove over to San Vicente Boulevard. In an eight-unit apartment building there, built around a blue tile pool, I found the apartment of Jean Talsman.

And Mary Cefalu, the mailboxes in the lobby informed me. That would be a paisan, Mary Cefalu, and I hoped she would like me better than she did Dora.

She was a tall girl and thin. She had a thin face with brown eyes as big as Italian olives and a thin-lipped wide mouth. She probably wouldn't qualify as pretty but she would attract all the truly masculine eyes within range.

"My name is Puma," I said.

She stood in the doorway of her apartment and looked at me without interest. "Is that supposed to mean something to me?"

"I guess not. I'm looking for Jean Talsman."

"Why?"

"She's missing. Do you know where she is?"

"I think I do. You're not the police, are you? God knows, you're big enough to be."

"In a way, I'm a policeman," I admitted, "though I'm licensed by the state." I took out the photostat of my license.

She looked at it and said, "A private detective. Good day to you, sir." She started to close the door.

"Wait!" I said sharply.

She stood there, the door half closed.

"I can come back with a policeman," I explained, "and he'll want to know what Jean was doing the night she disappeared. I'll have to tell them all about the engagement she had. And you'll make all the papers as her roommate. Now, Miss Cefalu, how much modeling work do you think you'll get after that happens?"

Her chin lifted. She looked like nothing below a duchess. "Are you presuming to threaten me, Mr. Puma?"

"Believe me, paisan, I'm not. I'm leveling."

"Dora Diggert sent you, didn't she? You're working for her."

"At the moment. I'm in business for myself, not Mrs. Diggert."

She stood in the doorway appraising me in indecision for seconds. Then she said quietly, "Come in."

The apartment was furnished in wrought iron and glass and bright nubby fabrics. The dining area overlooked the pool.

Mary Cefalu closed the door behind me and stood there, still skeptical. Then she asked, "Where are you from?"

"Fresno, originally," I answered. "Why?"

"You have that—peasant look. I'm from Tulare, myself."

"And you have that princess look," I said. "Well, that's the way the mop flops." I sighed.

She laughed and the room seemed warmer. She said, "I've just put some coffee on. Would you like a cup?"

"Thanks," I said, and went over to sit at the wrought-iron and glass table in the dining area.

She was in the kitchenette, reaching up for a cookie jar, when she said, "Dora and I don't get along. I blame Dora for what happened to Jean."

"You know what happened to Jean?"

She turned to stare at me. And then her face lightened. "Oh, I meant what happened—you know, why Jean got into—that line of work."

"I understand. Dora didn't twist her arm, did she?"

"No. But she introduced Jean to some of those cowtown billionaires and Jean is entirely too vulnerable to that kind of living."

"You mean she was used to living well?"

"About as much as you and I are. But she had a brother who got involved with the Syndicate and he began to live high off the hog. She thought a lot of that brother."

"And she went to work for Dora in rebellion?"

Mary Cefalu paused in the act of putting some cookies on a plate. "Maybe. You know, I never thought of it that way, but it could be . . ."

She brought the cookies over. The electric percolator on

the table was through perking and she poured us two cups of coffee.

"Cream?" she asked. "Sugar?"

"Neither, thank you," I said. "You told me before that you thought you knew where Jean was. Has she been in touch with you?"

"Not directly. Her brother phoned."

"Oh? And—"

"He was the man who was waiting for Jean at the Beverly Canyon Motel."

"God!" I said.

"What's the matter?"

"I was just thinking of how horrible that must have been. Imagine going to an assignation and discovering it's your brother waiting for you."

"He told me it was the only way he could get to talk with her. She hated him ever since he became a mobster. He thought the shame of her being discovered might make her listen to reason."

"He told you this on the phone?"

Mary Cefalu nodded.

"Do you know him? Did you recognize his voice?"

She shook her head. "I never met him. Jean has told me about him. Why did you ask that?"

"Because it means you can't be sure it was her brother who phoned. What did he tell you?"

"That he and Jean were going to Palm Springs for a couple of days."

"And why couldn't you have told Dora Diggert that when she called?"

Her thin face stiffened. "I wouldn't tell Dora Diggert anything. I despise that woman!"

I sipped my coffee and ate a cookie. I said, "It's phoney. If Miss Talsman was going to Palm Springs, she would have come home for some clothes, first. And she would have phoned you."

"She did come home for some clothes," Mary said. "That same night. I was out."

"In that case," I said, "this seems like a voluntary disappearance." I waited for her to look at me. "Do you think it is?"

She nodded, looking at me doubtfully. "If I didn't, I would have gone to the police yesterday."

The phone rang and she went to answer it. It was for me.

It was Dora Diggert. "That redhead from Ryerson's office just phoned me. You told her I'd sent you over there, didn't you?"

"That's right. I thought it would help to get me in to see Ryerson if I used your name."

"Well, the girl says she didn't tell the police you were sent by me. But she did tell them you talked with George this morning."

"The police—? What are they bothering her about?"

"Because George was just found dead, that's why. He was murdered."

TWO

DO THE POLICE know who did it?"

"The girl didn't say. And I imagine she has an angle in not giving them my name. The point is, Puma, can you keep my name out of it?"

"I don't know," I said honestly. "I'll try, Mrs. Diggert. I'd better call George's office right now."

I hung up and looked at Mary Cefalu. I said quietly, "George Ryerson has been killed. I questioned him this morning and the police will want to know why."

She stared at me. "So—?"

"If I tell them I was employed by Dora Diggert to locate Jean the police will know what Jean is. Do you want them to know that?"

She shook her head and continued to stare at me.

"But if I tell them you hired me, as Jean's roommate, the reasons why she went to the motel will never come out."

Mary asked, "You'd lie about that?"

"Wouldn't you, for Jean? Won't you?"

She nodded. "Of course." She took a deep breath. "I'm a little frightened, though."

I smiled at her. "Paisan, so am I. May I use your phone?"

She nodded absently and poured herself another cup of coffee.

I phoned George Ryerson's office and a voice I thought I recognized answered the phone.

"Joe Puma," I said efficiently, "calling George Ryerson."

"Is that so, Puma? And where are you now?"

It sounded like Sergeant Lehner, but I couldn't be sure. I asked, "To whom am I speaking?"

"The law, Puma. Sergeant Lehner. Where are you now?"

"At a client's apartment," I said. "Why?"

"The client that sent you over here this afternoon?"

"That's right, Sergeant. A Miss Mary Cefalu."

"And what's her connection with Ryerson?"

"There isn't any. Would you mind telling me what this is all about, Sergeant?"

"I'll tell you when I see you. Give me your client's address. And wait there for me."

I gave him Mary's address and went back to the wrought-iron table. I sat down and poured another cup of coffee.

Mary looked at me with a question in her eyes.

I said, "At least one officer is coming here, a Sergeant Lehner." I smiled reassuringly at her. "It's very simple. Jean was missing and you hired me to find her. Jean is a model, though she hasn't had much work in that field lately. The man she was to meet was a man named George Ryerson. But later, Jean's brother phoned and told you what he did. All of it is the truth except for the simple switch of clients."

"And Dora Diggert gets off the hook," Mary said bitterly.

"We're not thinking of her. We're thinking of Jean, aren't we? It's only Dora's good luck that we're thinking of Jean in this."

She sighed. "I guess. But I don't like it, somehow."

"It's all the truth," I insisted. "And you can tell them about Jean's brother, his tie-up with the mobs if you like. Tell them all the truth except the truth that will hurt Jean."

She stood up and stretched her long, taut body. She looked down at me thoughtfully. "Can I trust you, Joe Puma?"

"To the grave," I said.

She went to the kitchenette and came back with a bottle of Bushmills. "Join me?"

I nodded.

As she poured them, I said, "Remember, we don't know George Ryerson is dead. If Dora hadn't phoned, I wouldn't have known it, and we don't want her mentioned. So let them break that news."

"I'll remember," she said. She lifted her glass. "To luck."

We drank to that. We could use it in the next few hours.

Lehner came with another officer, but we never got to talk with him. Lehner did all the interrogating.

Mary gave him her story honestly and completely except for the single lie about being my client.

When she had finished, Lehner asked, "If her brother phoned, why were you still worried about her?"

Mary said evenly, "For two reasons. First, her brother is a hoodlum and I didn't like his story. And second, how could I be sure it was her brother?"

Lehner's thin, pugnacious face was bland. "I suppose you couldn't. And how did Miss Talsman happen to know Mr. Ryerson?"

"I have no idea. She has a number of friends we don't share."

"I see. What . . . uh . . . business did you say you were in, Miss Cefalu?"

"I didn't say. I'm a model. Coats, suits and hands."

"Uh-huh. Could you give me the names of some of the agencies you work for?"

Her chin lifted and her gaze was cool and candid. "Are you being insolent, Sergeant?" She was once more a countess.

He shook his head, studying her quietly.

She said in a cold, level voice, "I can give you the phone numbers of half a dozen major agencies I've worked for in the last two months. Would that be sufficient?"

"That would be fine," he said, and turned toward me. "Well, what's your story?"

"I was born in Fresno," I began, "of poor but proud Italian parents in the year—"

"Don't get smart, Puma," he said. "I want to know why you went to see Ryerson."

"Miss Cefalu has told you. And before I tell you anything, Sergeant, I want to know why we're being questioned. This is still America, despite your inflated opinion of yourself and your power."

The other man seemed to move closer. Lehner said softly, "Easy, Puma. You were never on my hit parade."

"A repugnance I reciprocate," I answered. "Let's go down to the station and talk to Captain Jeswald."

He stared and I stared and the other man muttered something. Finally, Lehner said, "I suppose it's your size that's made you so arrogant."

"My size and cops like you," I admitted.

"Officers," he corrected me.

"Officers like you," I said. "No matter what you may think of me, Sergeant, I'm still a citizen and helping to pay your salary. I think I warrant your respect."

He stared some more. If I had been fifty pounds lighter I might have been frightened.

Finally, he said, "Ryerson's dead."

"Murdered?"

He nodded.

"All right," I said. I settled back in my chair. "I was one of his visitors today. I asked him what business he'd had with Jean Talsman and he claimed he didn't even know her. I asked him if he had phoned her for one of his clients and he admitted that might be true. That was all he'd tell me."

"I see. And where was this engagement supposed to have taken place?"

I told him about the motel and my trip out there and the information I'd garnered from the desk clerk. And finished by saying, "So naturally I came back here to find out from Miss Cefalu if Jean's brother fit the description the desk clerk gave me of this man."

He looked at Mary. "Is there any picture of her brother around?"

"Not to my knowledge," she answered. "There might be, in one of her drawers."

Lehner's sardonic face turned my way again. "Was Ryerson registered at the motel?"

"Not by that name. Under the name of George Reimers."

He smiled cynically. "And the girl is a model, you say, like Miss Cefalu here?"

"I never compared her with Miss Cefalu," I said stiffly. "I never met her."

He stood up. "Well, with your permission, Miss Cefalu, we'll check the apartment for a picture of this brother. You may do it under our guidance if you prefer."

"Or you can refuse to," I explained to her, "unless they bring a warrant."

Lehner didn't look at me as he said, "That's correct."

"I'll do it," she said. "I've nothing to hide."

They went into the bedroom, leaving the other man with me. He sat down at the table and brought out a crumpled cigarette package. It was empty. He sighed.

I threw my pack across to him and said, "There's still some coffee. Want a cup?"

He glanced toward the other room and then smiled at me. "I guess." He picked up the cigarettes. "You and the sergeant aren't buddies, are you?"

"Even in the Department," I said, "he hasn't got any buddies." I poured him some coffee.

"You could be right," he said sadly, "and it's a damned shame. Because he's a very competent man."

"That's not enough, not today," I answered. "The bedside manner is important, too, today. You're new to plainclothes, aren't you?"

He nodded. "How'd you guess?"

"All the uniformed men are so polite in this town. It still sticks with you a little."

"Don't butter me, Puma," he said with a grin. "I don't like private men any more than he does."

I didn't argue with him. I asked, "How did Ryerson get it, and where?"

He frowned and glanced again toward the other room.

"For God's sake," I said, "it will be in all the papers in another half hour."

He smiled. "You can wait, then."

I leaned back and smoked and ignored him. He smoked my cigarette and drank Mary's coffee and ignored me.

George might have been a Syndicate kill but the Syndicate kills these days were very rare and never over the fate of a call girl. It would more likely be due to some shenanigans of George with the account of some maverick hood. The big boys can make all the money they need by using lawyers and accountants instead of torpedoes. Las

Vegas had set up the new semi-legal criminal element, the smooth boys who looked almost like human beings and who paid fifty thousand a week for single entertainers in their legalized clip-joints.

But to get back to my problem, the death of George Ryerson might possibly have nothing to do with the disappearance of Jean Talsman. The whole mix-up could have been simply an unfortunate coincidence.

Though for some reason I doubted that.

And the redhead . . . ? She had told me she'd never heard of Dora Diggert. Then how could she have phoned her at an unlisted number? She must have lied when we first met. Because Ryerson had done some income tax work for Dora and the redhead looked like one of those efficient girls who don't forget a client's name.

Sergeant Lehner came back into the room with Mary. He said to the other officer, "Nothing in there. And Miss Cefalu tells me there is no photograph anywhere in this room. We'll go out to that motel." He looked at me. "Come down and make out your report at your convenience, Mr. Puma. Any time within the next hour will be soon enough."

"Thanks, Sergeant," I said. "Remember me to the Captain."

"That I will," he promised. "I'll tell him all about you."

They left and Mary stood at the open doorway, staring at me. Then she closed the door and began to cry.

"Have another snort of that Bushmill's," I suggested. "Jean could be perfectly all right. This might have nothing to do with Jean."

She came back to sit at the table while I went to the phone to call Dora Diggert.

I told Dora, "Miss Cefalu had a phone call from a man who claimed he was Jean's brother. He said he and Jean were going to Palm Springs for a few days. So I guess you get one of your hundreds back."

"Not so fast, Puma. I hired you to find Jean, not dig up hearsay. You find her."

"I'd be getting into trouble, Ma'm," I said. "The law frowns on private men who get involved in homicides."

"Jean isn't involved in murder if she's in Palm Springs. And you've got to protect me, too, Puma."

"Protect you from what?"

"From the police."

"And the best way to do that," I pointed out, "would be for me to withdraw from the case this second. I'm involved with the police. But you, thanks to an assist from Miss Cefalu, are not."

"I don't need anything from Mary Cefalu. And what about that office girl of Ryerson's? What was her angle?"

"I don't know, but maybe some mild blackmail. I mean, she might want a little something for keeping your name out of the mess."

"Well, you find out what her angle is."

"All right," I said. "I'll check her and finish the day."

"And report back to me," she said crisply.

"Yes'm," I said meekly. "Yes'm, I'm on the way."

The station Lehner worked out of was Hollywood and I could get there easily from Ryerson's office. I decided that would be my schedule.

At the table, Mary stared at me tearfully.

"I won't leave until I'm sure you're all right," I offered.

The enormous brown eyes were brimming and her long, beautiful hands trembled on the glass table top. "Some of the men she knew," she said hoarsely, "some of the monstrous men she—" She inhaled heavily. "Jean was a—nice girl."

"I'm sure she's not in the past tense yet."

"I didn't mean that. And I didn't mean she was—is moral. Whatever that means. I meant she was generous and friendly and bright and fastidious. She—"

"So okay," I said. "This town is full of nice girls who get involved with swine. All towns are but this one more so, because there are more wealthy swine here. Let's not jump to any tragic conclusions, honey."

Mary put both hands to her temples. "But murder—? Oh, God!"

"The second that I locate Jean," I told her gently, "I'll insist that she phone you." And when, I asked myself, did I decide to continue looking for her?

Mary said, "You told Dora you weren't going to look any longer."

"I'll look because of you and Dora can pay for it. It's simple reciprocity after what you did for her."

She wiped her eyes and tried to smile. "Did I lie all right? I'm not very good at it, am I?"

"You were superb," I said. "Some night, could we go to a movie, or like that?"

She nodded gravely. "We could. Be careful, paisan."

"Okay, Tulare. And some other day, we'll take a trip up that way, won't we?"

She nodded. "My folks are still there. You have Jean phone me, hear? You tell her I think she's a fool."

I promised I would. I made a face at her and left.

The redhead was still at the office when I got back to Ryerson's. Her name, I learned, was Eileen Rafferty. She had recovered from the shock of Ryerson's death, she told me.

I said respectfully, "I had no idea you had been in shock, Miss Rafferty. You certainly showed poise in immediately phoning Dora Diggert."

She said heatedly, "I thought it was important. Don't you?"

"Both Dora and I do," I admitted. "We wondered why you did."

"Because George Ryerson has a lovely wife and two wonderful children. Why else?"

"That's what I'm trying to determine. You told the police about me. Weren't you afraid I might have to tell them I was working for Mrs. Diggert?"

She nodded. "I worried about it. But my first instinct was to protect Mrs. Ryerson and the children. Are you going to tell the police about Mrs. Diggert?"

"I may have to." I paused. "I'm thinking of Jean Talsman's reputation. We've told the police she was a model. She lives with a model."

Eileen Rafferty made no comment about that. She began to sort papers for filing.

I asked, "Any theories about what happened?"

She looked at me candidly. "George—Mr. Ryerson has always handled a number of, well—I suppose they could be called doubtful accounts. Not that everything wasn't legal, you understand?"

"Hoodlums' accounts, do you mean?"

She shrugged.

"How did that happen?"

"Well, he used to be a gambler, you know."

"George Ryerson—? That—"

"Square?" she supplied. "Yes. He's a whiz with figures. I mean he was. And right after he graduated from college, he thought he could invade Las Vegas with a system he and a friend had worked out. For almost a year, it looked like it would work. But then it began to fail them."

"For almost a year, in Las Vegas? Couldn't he retire on that?"

She shook her head. "You misunderstand. Any system that's based on sound mathematical principles is geared to show a very small profit over a long period of time. I mean a small percentage of profit. It requires a lot of money to show any worthwhile profit."

"You're quoting," I accused her.

She nodded. "I'm quoting George Ryerson. I heard that speech often enough."

"Maybe he planned to go back there and try it again."

"I don't think so. Some of the wheels around Vegas got interested in his experiment and that's how he got friendly with them. And when he opened this office, he convinced a number of them he could save them important money on their income taxes."

"And," I added, "keep them out of jail too."

She smiled acidly. "I didn't say it. Well, I'm about ready to lock up, Mr. Puma. Anything else?"

"Only the same question I asked before—any theories on who might have killed him?"

"None," she said.

"And will you be out of a job? Or will the firm continue?"

"The firm will continue. George had an order of succession all written up. He was a very careful man."

Not quite careful enough, I thought. I asked casually, "Did you know George—socially?"

She looked at me a moment before answering. Then: "I've been to his house for dinner. Is that what you meant?"

"I guess," I said. "Good luck, Miss Rafferty. Take care of yourself."

"I always have," she assured me.

At the station, I was told that Sergeant Lehner and his partner were not in, but I could dictate my statement to a stenographer and drop back to sign it after it had been typed.

That took less than half an hour and it was still too early to eat dinner. I was restless and irritable for no reason I could think of. This afternoon's violence had happened countless times before; murder was nothing new.

What had probably bothered me this afternoon was the public apathy toward hoodlums and the public support of this scum in such gilded cesspools as Las Vegas and Reno. Crime was now respectable; it was even admired.

I went up to the office and made out a report of the day's doings. From the office next door, I could hear the whir of Dr. Graves' drill and from the street below came the muted sounds of the fat-tired traffic on Beverly Drive.

We were in a money time again. Was that why I was so depressed: because I wasn't getting my slice of it? Why this adolescent petulance? I was a big boy and I had earned a hundred dollars today. I was no poet; I was a big, tough wop.

Suddenly my door opened and a man stood there. He was a big man. He stared at me without speaking.

"The washroom is at the end of the hall," I told him.

"Don't get smart, shamus," he said tightly.

I studied him, the breadth of his shoulders, the broken nose in the otherwise personable face, the costly tailoring and the clenched fists at his sides. I figured him to go about 190 pounds.

"What's your name?" I asked.

"Never mind that. Where's my sister?"

"If your name is Kelly," I said, "your sister's in Monaco. If your name is Falkenburg, she's in New York. If—"

"I warned you not to get smart, shamus. My name is Tom Talsman."

"Oh," I said, and stood up. "As far as I know, then, your sister is in Palm Springs. Maybe the police would know by this time. Shall I call Sergeant Lehner and ask him?" I reached for the phone.

He came over swiftly and clamped one big hand around my wrist.

We stood there glaring at each other like a pair of juvenile delinquents.

"You're big," I said reasonably, "but I'm bigger. Take your hand off my wrist or I'll belt you."

The back of his other hand came around to sting my cheek.

The rest I dislike to relate. My only excuse is the afternoon's depression and the peeve against hoodlums I had been building in my mind. I'm not normally pugilistic without cause.

He was holding my right wrist; I put my weight into the left I hooked in under his heart. He said "oof" and caught the edge of my mouth with a wild right hand.

I had turned now and he was still wavering from the hook. His back was to my desk and the route to his chin was unimpeded. I threw the big right hand.

He went down and the back of his head caught the edge of the desk with a sickening thunk. He was out before he hit the floor.

THREE

IT HAD BEEN a short battle. I stood there breathing hard, looking down at him and ashamed of the animosity bubbling in me. My office door was still open.

And from there, Dr. Dale Graves looked in to ask, "What the hell is going on in here, Joe?"

"My friend and I were trying some judo and he fell."

He looked at Tom Talsman on the floor and back at me. "Don't con me, Joe. Shall I call the police?"

"No," I said. A tooth had cut my lip; I could taste the blood in my mouth.

Dr. Graves said acidly, "Fearless Fosdick!" and went back to his office. I went to the cooler for a paper cup of water.

In a few seconds the sound of the drill resumed and the traffic was again audible on the street below. Tom Talsman didn't stir and I couldn't tell if he was breathing. I set the cup of water on the edge of my desk and knelt beside him, feeling for a pulse.

There was a pulse and I stood up again, rubbing my aching right hand.

He moaned finally and his eyes slowly opened. I knelt again and held the cup of water to his lips. He paused only a second before drinking it.

Uncertainly, he got to his feet. He stood quietly a moment, rubbing the back of his head. "You're a lucky son-of-a-bitch," he said.

"That's my history. Had enough, Mr. Talsman?" I smiled. "I mean enough water, of course."

"I've had enough water. I'm not through with you, though, shamus. When I get my bearings, we might go around once more."

"Why?" I asked. "What's your beef with me, Talsman?"

"You tell me," he said bitterly. "A man is killed and my sister disappears and the police grill you about it. It's been my experience that when a private eye is mixed up in a mess like that, he's usually at the bottom of it. I know your breed."

"Easy, now," I warned him. "I don't like any kind of hoodlum, either. Pushers or pimps or gamblers or guns or fixers or frauds, I don't like any of 'em. And I can take you again and again and again; have no illusions about that. You came here and asked a question and I was courteous enough to offer you the best answer I had. If you have any more polite questions, ask 'em."

His palm massaged the back of his head. He looked around and saw my customer's chair and went over to sit in it. He stared at me doubtfully. "That was one hell of a lucky punch."

I said nothing.

"Who's Jean with now?" he asked.

"Believe me, I haven't the faintest idea. I was sent to find her and the best description I have of the man she met is this: He was a fairly short, stocky man with a full head of black hair and he was dressed in the kind of clothes George Raft used to wear. That could be any one of a number of hoodlums. It's the description I got from the desk clerk at the Beverly Canyon Motel."

He appraised me quietly.

I said, "It must be a man who knew she worked for Dora Diggert and who knew George Ryerson and who also knew you and Jean were not friendly. He used your name when he phoned Jean's roommate and he said they were going to spend a few days in Palm Springs. Jean must have gone with him willingly because she came back to the apartment for some clothes when her roommate was out.

"What makes you think Jean and I weren't friendly?"

"Just hearsay," I answered. "I heard she resented your going into the rackets and assumed she might have gone into her—profession as a sort of rebellion. Could that be possible?"

He had the grace to color. "Who knows?"

"Well, were you friends?"

"That wouldn't be your business," he said.

"No, it wouldn't," I agreed. "And gassing with you wouldn't be profitable, either, but that's what I've been doing. Good-by to you, glass jaw."

He asked quietly, "How tough are you against a gun?"

"As tough as my .38 and my luck can keep me. Nobody lives forever." I went over to sit behind my desk. "Now beat it before I call the police."

He stood up. "You'll see me again, Dago."

"Wait," I said, and came out from behind the desk. "That word. You didn't mean it, did you?"

He turned around to look at me. After a second, he said, "I didn't mean it. I've still got a few rattles in my brain. We'll meet again."

As soon as I heard his feet going down the stairs, I phoned Mary Cefalu. I told her about his visit and said, "He may be on his way to see you right now."

"He was here an hour ago," she answered. "Was I wrong in giving him your name, Joe?"

"No, that was all right. I—worried about you."

"You're sweet," she said. "You're a typical Fresno fig."

I hung up and leaned back in my chair. Then I remembered I was to phone Dora Diggert and I tried her. A phone answering service informed me that Mrs. Diggert was not momentarily available but would phone me back when she was reached.

I was lighting a cigarette when Dr. Graves came in.

"Just what I'm looking for," he said.

I gave him the pack and the matches.

He glanced at the floor. "I see you've removed the body. Where'd you dump him, Fosdick?"

"He walked out. Tell me, do professional men also get

this unholy urge to swing on people every once in a while?"

"Everybody does. These are trying times, Joe. I guess you Latins are a little quicker on the trigger, but I'd bet almost any active person today comes close to murder now and then."

"No," I argued. "Suicide, but not murder."

"Suicide is murder." He smiled. "It even insures the death penalty. Pretty good crack, huh?"

"For a molar-grinder, I suppose. Do you like your job, Dale?"

He shrugged. "I imagine there are worse. Why'd you ask?"

"I've been on the hunt for a missing call girl, all afternoon."

He chuckled. "Well, I'll grant you I'd rather be a call boy, but I haven't the charm. What do you do when you find her?"

"Not what you're thinking. That was her brother, here on the floor. He's a hoodlum. And yet the girl is pretty and the brother was certainly big and handsome and not dumb. What twists them?"

"I don't know either one of them so I couldn't say. What got you on this kick? You're usually more pragmatic, Puma."

I shrugged.

He asked smilingly, "Do you like your job, Joe?"

"At times. At rare times."

The phone rang, and I answered it. It was Dora. Dale went out as I explained to Dora about my talk with Eileen Rafferty and my visit from Jean's brother.

"Didn't I tell you?" she said smugly. "Jean isn't with her brother. That means she's in danger."

"Maybe. Maybe not."

"Well, you find out, Joseph Puma. If she's in Palm Springs, you go there."

"Yes'm," I said wearily. "That will swell the expenses. Meals are expensive in Palm Springs."

"Find her," she said sharply, and hung up.

My lower lip was bulging around the small cut. I tried to make sense out of the things that had happened today and very little sense came to mind. A man had used a C.P.A. to make a date with a girl and had later changed his false identity to the girl's brother. That looked like kidnapping—except that the girl had gone along willingly. Or so it seemed. And the C.P.A. had been murdered.

A nice clear and clean-cut case and it shouldn't take too long to unravel. Maybe twenty, twenty-five years?

Everybody had lied. Was the Palm Springs bit another lie? And if it wasn't, that was still a flimsy lead. Palm Springs isn't a big town but it's too big a town to locate a person without an address.

And why the brother angle? Could it be a way to smoke the real brother out of hiding? And why was George Ryerson killed?

I didn't even know where, but the late editions would be out now with all the information Sergeant Lehner's sidekick had refused to divulge to me. I picked up a *Herald-Express* on my way to dinner at Cini's Italian Restaurant.

There, over my pizza, I read about the death of George Ryerson. He had been found in his car, a bullet through his temple, on a huge free parking lot in the Bluffview shopping center. He usually ate in Beverly Hills, according to his receptionist, and she had no idea what business could have sent him to the Bluffview area.

After a visit from an unidentified private investigator, Miss Rafferty continued, Mr. Ryerson had been obviously agitated and had broken an appointment for lunch made only that morning with an important client. The murder weapon was identified as .25 calibre and a bore that small would almost need a temple shot to prove fatal. No gun had been found.

I was familiar with the Bluffview shopping center and its parking lot. It was different from most of the others out here, where the rear windows of all the business buildings usually look out over the parking lot. The Bluffview lot was effectively screened by rows of eucalyptus along its borders and if a man wanted a public place to commit murder, a better spot would be difficult to find.

But why would a murderer choose any kind of public spot? Unless it had been an unpremeditated act?

Not that any of it was my concern; my sole mission was to find Jean Talsman. Ryerson's death might or might not be connected with Jean's disappearance. Though the fact that he had cancelled a luncheon appointment after my visit could indicate he had gone out to Bluffview to meet someone because of my call. One of his hoodlum clients? They wouldn't be likely to use a .25 calibre weapon. That seemed more like the work of some errant teen-ager.

I told myself Ryerson's death was none of my business but it continued to bother me.

I finished eating and phoned Mary Cefalu. I told her, "I've been eating pizza and thinking about you."

"Monster!" she said. "While I've been eating beans."

"I was thinking about Jean, too," I went on. "I was thinking it would be a wild goose chase to run out to Palm Springs without more of a lead than I have now. I wondered if there couldn't be some information you overlooked, some name she has mentioned that might make the trip worthwhile."

"I've been thinking, too," she said. "You know, Jean has a fair voice and an urge to be an entertainer. If somebody was going to con her into a Palm Springs trip, that could be the angle. When her brother was here, he mentioned a man named Jack Ross. Have you ever heard of him?"

"Vaguely. Doesn't he run a night spot in Palm Springs?"

"Yes. A gambler, I think, isn't he?"

"I guess." I hesitated and then said, "Why don't we run out there for the weekend?"

A pause. "I'm—not one of Dora's girls, Mr. Puma."

"I know, I know. We'd get separate rooms and I'd charge them both to Dora. I thought you might have more luck questioning Jean than I would, that's all."

Another pause and she asked doubtfully, "Are you sure that's all you had in mind?"

"It's not all I had in mind," I admitted, "but it's all I'll expect. Any further advances would have to come from you."

"Well," she said musingly, "I've really nothing to lose, have I?"

I told her I'd pick her up in half an hour and then I phoned a motel I was familiar with in Palm Springs and reserved a pair of rooms. It was a fairly new motel with a man-sized pool and a pleasant bar, a fine place to combine business with pleasure.

I picked up some clothes, including my swimming trunks, before driving over to Mary's apartment.

When I arrived she was ready, wearing a faille suit that demonstrated why she modeled suits, a big smile and an air of impending adventure.

"You look about eighteen years old," I said. "Is the prospect of seeing Jean again that exciting?"

She made a face at me. "Let's get on the road, paisan. And remember, no passes."

I picked up her bag. "Consider me a eunuch."

"Never," she promised. "What really makes me happy is knowing Dora will be paying for it all."

I didn't want to spoil her fun; I let her believe that.

We didn't see much of the desert; it was dark by the time we got to it. In the little Plymouth, the music came softly from the radio and the faint odor of Mary's perfume lightened the night air.

"Could we get a place with a pool?" she asked.

"I've already reserved the rooms. The pool's one of the biggest in the town. I wonder if this Jack Ross is our man?"

"He could easily be. I know Dora hates him and that might be the reason he used the name of Jean's brother when he phoned me. He didn't want Dora interrupting the —the *rendezvous?*"

"That's as good a word as any," I said. "This whole thing is so screwy, I get the feeling I'm due to wake up any minute."

Mary said thoughtfully, "Well, what other way could he get in touch with Jean if he didn't know her address? And he didn't. He had this Ryerson person phone Dora because he must have learned that Ryerson had Dora as an account. And then, to get Ryerson off the hook and still not reveal anything to Dora, he used Tom Talsman's name. Or that might even have been Jean's idea."

"Then why didn't Jean phone you and save you the worry?"

"I don't know. But using her brother's name like that would make me feel everything was all right. I mean, they could have figured that."

"Maybe. It's too confusing."

"Let's not think about anything but those big steaks Dora is going to pay for. And the fine desert sun and the big pool. Let's forget George Ryerson, shall we?"

We rode in silence for a while. I don't know what Mary was thinking about, but I couldn't get my mind off the subject of George Ryerson, husband and father. The logical niche for him was simply as an agent who had performed a minor service for a client, getting him a readily available girl. And not even for the girl's usual service. So far as I knew now.

Why, then, should Ryerson die? What swift and awful emotion had possessed the killer?

I asked, "How long was Jean in this business?"

Mary sighed. "About six months. She used to sing a little in some of the cheaper places on the Strip and in the beach towns. And then she had a dry spell and during that time she met Dora. Dora is like a—heavens, I was going to say like a mother to her. Most mothers wouldn't sell their daughters, would they?"

"Not in Fresno or Tulare," I said. "Was—is Jean a hundred dollar girl?"

"She never told me about her rates. But I heard she got as high as a thousand from one of those romantic Texans."

Silence again. Across the flat wasteland, headlights appeared miles up the road and took minutes to reach us and rush past. The night was clear; the stars were out and an edge of the moon was peeking over the rim of the black mountains.

"That desert air," Mary said. "Isn't it clean?"

"Most uninhabited places are clean," I said.

"Let us not be cynical," she said mockingly. She lighted a cigarette and asked, "One for you?"

"Please."

Silence again. I thought of Eileen Rafferty and about her call to Dora. I thought of the pugnacious Tom Talsman and wondered if he was now in Palm Springs. None of this thinking seemed to be getting me anywhere so I thought of the evening ahead.

The manager of the motel was behind the desk when I entered the office about nine o'clock. Mary had stayed in the car, and the manager smirked as he said, "Flanking rooms, Joe. With a connecting door. One of the units has a kitchenette."

"It's nothing like that," I protested.

"You can keep the door locked then," he said dryly. "Business bring you to town?"

"I'm looking for a man named Jack Ross," I explained. "And a woman named Jean Talsman."

"Ross, I know," he said, "if it's the man who runs the Blue Lantern."

"I imagine it is. The girl's name doesn't ring a bell though?"

He shook his head.

I asked, "And what kind of a man is Ross?"

"Very solid for a man with his background. He used to be a gambler, you know. Might still be, for all I know."

"I see. Do you remember another former gambler, a man named George Ryerson?"

He frowned and shook his head slowly. His frown deepened and he reached over to pick a *Mirror-News* from the rack next to the desk. He tapped the paper. "This George Ryerson?"

I nodded.

"Never met him," he said musingly, "but Ross could have. Ross used to live in Las Vegas. This Ryerson was a kind of boy wonder math wizard a few years back, wasn't he? Had a system at Vegas?"

"That's the man," I admitted.

He stared at me. "You don't think Ross might have—" He didn't finish.

I shrugged.

Then, from the doorway, Mary said, "What's keeping you, Joe? Do I have to register for myself?"

"I'll be right there," I promised. "Rooms eighteen and twenty. You take the one with the kitchenette."

She went away. The manager smiled. "I'll bet you'll keep the door locked. Man, you do pick the winners, don't you?"

I said stiffly, "I brought her along to identify the girl I'm looking for. Now, that's enough of that."

He was reading the *Mirror-News* as I went out with the keys. He was still smiling.

I explained to Mary, "The connecting door wasn't anything I asked for. I suppose he always keeps it to the last in case a family of more than three comes along."

"It's all right," she said. "It has a lock."

"As soon as I've shaved," I told her, "we'll run over to the Blue Lantern. That's the name of Ross's place."

"Could we eat, too?" she asked. "Those beans weren't very filling."

"You can eat. I had the pizza, remember?"

As I shaved, I noticed that the cut in my lip had turned dark and there was a stiffness along that side of my mouth. I soaked it in warm, soapy water and dried it tenderly. Looking at myself in the mirror, I was forced to face myself. And facing myself, I was forced to admit it had been a very flimsy lead that had brought me to Palm Springs. But I was sorely in need of a day in the sun; I would have come for even less reason than I had.

From the next room, Mary called, "Let's move, man. I'm anxious to talk with Jean."

I put on my jacket and came out of the bathroom. The connecting door was open and Mary stood there, smiling at me. I said carefully, "We can't be positive she's in Palm Springs."

"We'll never learn, standing here," she said. "Let's go."

We went out into a night so clear it was almost a theatrical setting, each star unblinking in the blue-black sky, the big white moon apparently tied to the Royal Palm that towered over the motel office.

"If we were rich," Mary said with a sigh, "we could spend the whole winter here."

"Together, do you mean? Living in sin?"

"Don't be vulgar. I meant it generally, not specifically. Is the Blue Lantern far? Could we walk over?"

I went into the office and asked the manager and he told me it was only a three block walk. So we didn't take the car. We walked along the quiet street and I was happy to be here, even if we never found Jean Talsman.

The Blue Lantern was one of the older buildings, Spanish, with wrought-iron spears supporting the awning over the entrance, a heavy tile roof, and a flagstone court around the fountain in the patio section. We went past a dim bar to the equally dim dining room, and were met there by a stocky man with a heavy head of shiny black hair and George Raft tailoring.

"You're Jack Ross," I guessed.

He shook his head and smiled pleasantly. "Would you like to speak with Mr. Ross?"

"Please," I said.

But Mary said, "There's Jean now, Joe." And to the head waiter, "Never mind about Mr. Ross. We've found the person we came to see."

In a corner booth, a girl who matched the picture I had was sitting with a tall, sandy-haired man near middle age. The man rose as we approached the booth.

Jean was smiling and Mary was bubbling and the sandy-haired man said genially, "Welcome to the Blue Lantern. My name is Jack Ross."

In the next half hour I learned that Ross had caught Jean's act on the Strip a few times and had met her at a few parties. They had become casual friends but when he had thought of hiring her to work at his place, Dora had refused to give him Jean's address or phone number. Then, one day, he'd brought his books in to George Ryerson for outside auditing and he had seen Dora in the outer office. George had admitted that Dora was a client.

So George had phoned for him, arranging the date.

"And you met her at the motel?" I asked him.

He shook his head. "I couldn't get away. So I sent my *maitre d'* in to convince her this was a much sounder future."

"And he phoned to tell Mary that Jean was with her brother?"

"To pacify Dora," Ross explained. "She is no Jack Ross fan."

"Oh—?"

He smiled. "Was that a question?"

"Not unless you want to answer it."

"Well," he said slowly, "I . . . almost married Dora. That was a few years back. I . . . learned some . . . I mean, it didn't come off."

"You wouldn't care to tell me why?"

He shook his head. "No, I wouldn't."

I studied him. He had freckles under his desert tan. He had honest, light blue eyes and an engaging grin and a comfortable, pleasant personality. He could have been twenty or fifty; he wasn't the kind who aged.

"And what about Ryerson?" I asked. "Why did he die?"

He said solemnly, "I haven't the faintest idea. He handled the accounts of some . . . gentlemen I wouldn't want to do business with. It might have been that he crossed one of them. I'm sure that Jean's disappearance at the same time was an unfortunate coincidence."

In the subdued light, I looked at Jean Talsman. The picture had made her look younger but she was a beautiful girl and the defiance that had intrigued me in the picture was visible tonight.

Ross said, "Everything is on the house."

"A New York cut, rare," Mary said quickly.

I asked Jean, "Have you heard from your brother?"

She shook her head, staring at me. "Why do you ask that?"

I told her about his visit to Mary and his tangle with me. "He mentioned Ross's name to Mary so I assumed he knew you were here."

Jean looked worriedly at Ross and he sighed. Nobody said a word for seconds.

Then Mary said, "To hell with Tom Talsman. Order champagne, Joe."

"When it's free," I said, "I'll take Jack Daniel's Tennessee whisky. But I'll still worry about Tom Talsman." I looked at Jean. "And with reason, wouldn't you agree?"

Jean didn't answer. There was another silence.

Then Jack Ross said, "You're not suggesting Jean's brother might have killed Ryerson, are you?"

"No. Though it isn't impossible, now that you mention it. He implied he'd have a gun with him next time he ran into me." I looked again at Jean. "Does his reputation make that a reasonable threat?"

She nodded slowly.

Our drinks came and the man at the Hammond organ weaved some intricate improvisations around "Deep Purple."

I asked Jack Ross, "Do you still gamble?"

He smiled. "When I can find a game that seems worth the effort. Not for a living, I don't. I lost two-thirds of the money my dad left me, learning to gamble."

"Is that when you met George Ryerson, when you were gambling?"

He nodded, and said, "I even tried out his system for four nights. And lost thirty thousand dollars."

Mary's steak came and more Jack Daniels came and the dialogue shifted to other things, to the Texas floods and

Liberace's suit against the scandal magazine. Some other people came whom Mary knew and we took a bigger table out in the court, where the fountain glistened under the colored spotlights.

I don't remember their names, but it was all a lot of fun and I didn't think of George Ryerson once. I thought of Dora, but decided I would phone her in the morning.

As we walked back to the motel in the cold desert night, Mary said, "That Jack Ross is serious about Jean, isn't he?"

"He seems to be. Tolerant, too, eh?"

Silence for about five steps. Then, "What did that mean?"

"Mary, I'm not rapping the girl. She's very attractive. And bright, too. But I mean, this Ross seems to come from a good family and Jean was—is—well—"

"A call girl," she finished for me. "And you're a call boy. But that's different, I suppose?"

"You're being obscure," I said. "How am I a call boy?"

"All men are," she explained. "Any attractive girl can get any man for an evening if he knows she's—well, available. You wouldn't even expect to be paid. You'd come for nothing."

"Nonsense," I said.

"I'm being truthful, and it hurts. Men are so damned narrow and superior about morality. It's a one-way street with them."

I took her hand. "Let's not fight. We had such a fine evening. Let's be friends."

She sighed. "Wasn't it wonderful? And won't it be wonderful for Jean, married to that nice man?"

"That nice, rich man," I qualified it.

"All right. Yes. It helps that he's rich. You're not against that, too, are you?"

I didn't answer. I thought of the too frequent characterization of rich people being bored. How could a man be bored with a tableful of congenial friends and a cupboard full of Jack Daniels? If he would be bored with that, he would be desolate, poor.

At the doorway to her room, Mary asked, "Am I in any danger? Should I keep that connecting door locked?"

I bent over and kissed her forehead. "Suit yourself, lady. It has been a lovely evening; I want for nothing."

She put her slim fingers to my lips and went into her room.

While I was taking my shower, I could hear hers running. Not that I was expecting any windfalls, but I added a dash of manly cologne to my own ministrations.

She was a lovely girl. She was friendly and unaffected and very fashionable and long-limbed and high breasted and her companionship alone would be enough to make any reasonable man happy.

I lay in the dark room thinking back on the day. It had sure as hell been a wing-dinger. This was the first interesting case in months, after a dreary succession of hotel skips and errant husbands. This was the kind of case the TV investigators ran into constantly.

I lay in the dark room, wondering.

And then, when I heard the first creak of the connecting door opening, I thought it would add the properly light touch to inquire innocently, "Who's there?"

FOUR

IN THE MORNING, I smelled coffee. The door was open between the rooms and I put on a robe to go over and saw Mary opening a carton of eggs.

"What time is it?" I asked her. "Where'd you get all the groceries?"

"It's ten-thirty, lazy man. I got the eggs at a store. That pool is just waiting for some occupants."

I shook my head. "A typical Tulare peasant—up at ten-thirty. How are you feeling?"

She looked at me speculatively. "How should I feel?"

"After all the liquor, I meant. What else could I mean?"

"I wasn't sure, but you can stop being paternal. How do you like your eggs?"

"I'll fix 'em," I said. "Nobody else can fry them the way I like them."

She handed me the pan. "Okay, mama's boy; you can fix mine, too."

This was Saturday morning and Mary had brought back a Los Angeles morning newspaper from the grocery store. I read what there was about the murder in the paper but there was nothing I didn't know. Except that George Ryerson's widow had sought a divorce a few months back and had then withdrawn the action.

Would that indicate she had a lover? No. But if it did, the lover could be a prime suspect for George's murder.

"What are you thinking about?" Mary asked.

"About George Ryerson. His death bothers me. Now why should that be?"

She looked at her coffee. "Perhaps because you read that he had been agitated after your visit and had broken a luncheon engagement." She looked at me. "Maybe that made you feel sort of responsible for his death."

After a moment, I said, "I don't think that's it."

"You certainly wouldn't want to think that's it. Finish your coffee and let's get out into the sun."

"You run along," I said. "I have to phone Dora and report. I'll be out in a few minutes."

I phoned from my room, with the door closed. Dora answered almost immediately.

I told her, "I've located Jean Talsman. She is going to sing at a restaurant here in Palm Springs. The place is owned by a man named Jack Ross. The rumor is that they're romantically involved, too."

"I'll bet. And why didn't she tell me any of this before?"

"I don't know, Mrs. Diggert. I asked her to phone you and she wouldn't promise, but I have a feeling she will."

Silence for a few seconds and then Dora said bitterly, "She's a fool! That man is no good for her."

I said nothing.

"He's a spoiled, petulant ass, pretentious, affected—"

I didn't argue.

"Puma, are you still there?"

"Yes'm," I said. "I guess that finishes me up on the case. It all happened in one day, but it was a long day."

"You're not through," she told me. "I want you to get her promise to phone me. Can you do that?"

"I can try."

"Well, try! And tell her she doesn't have to go out on calls. I have plenty of other work for a girl of her intelligence."

"I'll tell her if I get her alone."

"Why can't you get her alone?"

"She and Jack—Mr. Ross, I mean, are together most of the time, the way I understand it."

"How touching! You know he's a hoodlum, don't you? He's a gambler."

"I know he was a gambler. I didn't know he was or is a hoodlum."

"It's the same thing and you're too bright to split hairs over the terminology. You get her to phone me, Puma."

"I'll try. Good-bye, Mrs. Diggert."

The click of her phone was my good-bye. Dora was annoyed.

Why . . .? What difference could it make to Dora if Jean was involved with a gambler? Was that any less moral than going out on calls? And if Jean was no longer going out on calls, it couldn't be Dora's loss of commission that was troubling her.

I put on my trunks and went out to the pool. Mary was sitting on the diving board in a simple number of black lastex, trying to get a rubber cap over her long black hair. In the bright sunlight, her hair shone like polished jet.

"We live in a matriarchy," I said sourly. "And Dora Diggert is one of its queens."

"She's a slob. Help me with this cap, will you? Damn it, I'm going to cut my hair short!"

"Not while I'm your favorite, you're not. Here, I'll fix it for you." I went up onto the board and it began to sag dangerously.

Mary looked at my pillar legs and sighed. "What a hunk of meat you are."

"You're pretty, too." I tucked the side strands in under the cap. "Why do you hate Dora Diggert so much?"

"Because of what she did to Jean, of course. Why else?"

I took a breath. "Jean was of age, wasn't she? And sound in mind and body. It's absurd to blame Dora for that."

The big eyes began to harden as she stared at me. I put a hand on her shoulder and pushed.

She went into the water with a monumental splash and came up sputtering. I dove her way and stayed under, looking for her legs.

The water was clear: she could see me coming. One

of her long legs kicked out when I came within range and I got up holding my nose.

It was numb but not bleeding.

She said sharply, "Don't manhandle me! Don't ever manhandle me!"

"Right," I said quietly. I dove under the surface and swam leisurely away.

At the shallow end, I waded out and went up to the deck. I lighted a cigarette and stared off toward the highway. I could hear her splashing in the pool but I didn't look at her. With a touch of corny drama, I put a careful finger to my nose and then studied the finger, searching for blood. I hoped she was watching.

The splashing stopped and I heard her wet feet padding along the hot concrete. A towel dropped next to me and in a second she did, too. I thoughtfully studied the sparse traffic on the highway.

"You're sulking," she said.

I shook my head.

A silence and then, "It goes way back to something that happened in Tulare. I'm sorry. It's a—phobia?"

I shrugged indifferently.

"All right," she said. "All right! Three hundred pounds of brooding sensitivity. You should see how silly you look—"

"Not quite three hundred pounds, thank you," I said. "And my sensitivity goes back to something that happened in Fresno—my birth."

Silence . . . and I turned to look at her. She was staring at the water and she seemed sad and lost.

"I'm sorry," I said. "I was teasing. Kiss me, please?"

"People are watching. What will they think?"

"They'll think the truth, I suppose. Would you like a cigarette?"

She leaned over quickly and kissed me on the cheek. "Joe, why I hate Dora, it seemed to me that her—I mean, it seemed like a deliberate campaign, the way she got Jean into that—business. It seemed so monstrously premeditated, if you follow me?"

"Couldn't you argue Jean out of taking the big step?"

She sighed and wiped the water from her face with the back of a hand. "I didn't even know she'd taken it until three months later. I should have suspected, I suppose, the kind of dates she had, and hours she came in, drunk more often than not."

I lighted a cigarette and handed it to her. "You make it sound like Dora was charting a planned degradation for the girl. Now, why in hell would anyone do that?"

"I've no idea. Have you? You're the detective."

"You're bound to be biased," I said, "by your sentiment for Jean. You could be just as wrong about her as you might be about Dora. When will we be seeing Jean today?"

"This afternoon. Why?"

"I've got a message for her."

"Joe, you're not going to ask her to phone Dora? Please?"

"Don't interfere in my business, Mary. I won't manhandle you and you don't interfere in my business."

"It has nothing to do with business. It's a simple question of decency, of morality."

"That question, kid, was answered by Jean herself, months ago."

Another one of our frequent silences. Mary looked at me sadly and I smiled at her.

"Bull-headed wop," she said finally.

"Both of us," I added. "I don't want to fight, but I don't want to be interfered with, either, not in my trade."

"So all right already," she said. "Would you get me a Coke from the machine?"

Lovers' squabbles under the desert sun. And in Los Angeles, George Ryerson's body would be ready for burial now. Nobody I had met seemed to be mourning him. But I hadn't met his widow or his children.

At noon, Jean phoned and invited us to the Blue Lantern for dinner. Mary told her we had eaten breakfast at 10:30, so Jean suggested a four o'clock dinner, and why didn't we come over earlier for some gab and drinks? I agreed that would be fine.

We swam some more, played a dozen torrid games of table tennis, then went in to get ready for our free meal. This was developing into the most pleasant case of my ignoble career.

It was cool in the court of the Blue Lantern; refrigerated blowers ringed the walls all around. The fountain glistened and gurgled and the waiter served wine coolers. This kind of living would be a long step up for Jean. A girl today can go almost anywhere if she's pretty and properly endowed and not too dumb.

Jean Talsman said, "What are you thinking about, Joe Puma?"

"Women," I said. "It's a woman's world."

Ross winked. "I second that."

Jean said "Huh!" and Mary sniffed.

I said, "I promised Dora I'd ask you to phone her. I'm asking you now, officially."

She smiled. "I might. I've a few things I'm aching to tell her."

"Nothing you'd want to tell me?"

"Nothing. I'm beyond pettiness. I've found a handsome man with money and I'm going to turn tolerant and kind."

The fountain tinkled, the blowers hummed, the wine coolers warmed us while cooling. Footsteps sounded in the deserted restaurant and grew louder as they approached the flagstone of the court.

A man came into view beyond the fountain. He was a fairly big man with a broken nose in an acceptable face and it seemed obvious to me he was drunk. And belligerent.

Jean said softly, "It's Tom and he's drunk. I wonder what he wants from us?"

Ross said calmly, "We'll soon find out."

Talsman saw us then and headed our way, walking carefully and with a disciplined minimum of waver. He came to within a few feet of the table and stared at his sister.

He said thickly, "Let's get out of here, Jean. This is no place for you."

Jean said bitterly, "Isn't it a little late for you to be showing concern for your baby sister?"

He swayed. "You may not know it, but you're sitting with a killer, Sis. Come on, we're going."

Jean's eyes widened but she looked at no one but her brother.

I asked casually, "Who's the killer, Talsman?"

He glanced at me and then at Ross. Still looking at Ross, he said to me, "Ask him."

"I have no idea what you're talking about," Ross said, "and I'm sure you haven't either. You're drunk, boy."

"A little," Talsman admitted. "Who else had enough on Ryerson to make him pull what he did, use his name to get to my sister?"

Ross said, "I was in this town the entire afternoon of the day Ryerson was killed. I can call a number of substantial citizens who will testify to that."

"With your kind of money," Tom Talsman said, "any kind of witness can be bought. Jean, I'm thinking about you."

"It would be the first time in your life," his sister said. "Please go, Tom. You're being ridiculous."

He nodded and smiled owlishly. He reached into a jacket pocket and brought out a revolver. It looked like a .32. It moved casually around at the four of us.

"Come along, Jean," he said hoarsely.

The court was deserted: no waiter was in sight. All of us stared at the moving revolver.

Jean said shakily, "Please, Tom? Believe me, I know Jack had nothing to do with Ryerson's death."

Ross said earnestly, "You're making a serious mistake about me. I'm sure, if you give me the chance, I can prove that."

"Jack and I are going to be married, Tom," Jean put in.

He shook his head. "You'll never marry a murderer, not while I'm alive."

I thought it was about time to stop being polite. So I said, "Talsman, put that gun away. You're in more trouble already than you can handle. Don't compound it."

The gun swung my way and Tom Talsman looked at me calmly. "Make a move, big boy. The bore is small, but the bullets are hollow-point."

Behind him, now, I could see a waiter in the entry to the dining room. The waiter was watching us and now he beckoned to another waiter.

I talked slowly, keeping Talsman's attention on me. "If I made a move, you would undoubtedly pull the trigger. You would then be a murderer. And how would that help?"

The waiter was moving up from behind as quietly as all good waiters move.

Talsman said, "Big mouth private eye. You were gutty enough yesterday, weren't you? What happened to your guts? Make the move."

I smiled at him. "Not against hollow-points. They make too big a hole."

He nodded. "Didn't I warn you last time we met that—"

It was as far as he got. The waiter was directly behind him and he had reached out swiftly to grab Talsman's right arm. As he reached, I came up out of my chair, bringing the swinging right hand up in the same forward motion.

For the second time in the historic Talsman-Puma matches, I was on target. My right fist found the button as Talsman twisted away from the waiter. The gun clattered along the flagstones as he went back and down.

Mary gasped, Jean shrieked and the waiter said quietly, "I'll phone the police."

"That won't be necessary," Jack Ross said quickly. "The boy was drunk and nobody has been hurt."

On the flagstones, Talsman put a hand behind him to lift himself to a sitting position. I had the gun now.

I said to Ross, "He's no boy and he came here armed. I think you're making a mistake."

Tom Talsman stood up and rubbed the back of his head. "Ross doesn't want any law around here. That's the last thing he wants."

"Do you?" I asked Talsman. "You're free to swear out a complaint."

Talsman said nothing, staring at me contemptuously.

The headwaiter was coming over now, the stocky man with the glossy hair. He said firmly, "Mr. Ross, I think it would be more sensible for all of us, if we phoned the police."

Ross looked at Jean and back at the headwaiter. I could guess that he was thinking about his fiancée and the news that would break in the papers about the girl Ryerson was supposed to have met coming to Palm Springs and getting involved in gun play. That was probably the reason he said, "If nobody objects more seriously than that, I'm not going to phone." He looked around. "Unless someone insists."

Silence, as he gazed at each of us in turn. And then he turned to Talsman. "You had better go quietly now. Unless you are willing to listen to reason?"

Talsman said, "Not your reasons." He turned his back on us and walked toward the gate leading to the street.

Jean started to cry and Ross looked hopelessly at me. Mary moved over to sit next to Jean. Tom Talsman was now out of sight. The ineffectual hoodlum, I thought. This makes his second unsuccessful intimidation attempt in two days. He had better get into another line of work.

I said, "Poor Tom. He's always winding up on his back."

Jean stopped crying long enough to tell me, "Don't underestimate him, Mr. Puma."

"Let's forget him," I suggested. "He was drunk and unreasonable and possibly dangerous. But he's gone, now."

Ross handed Jean a handkerchief and she blew her nose. Mary glared at me. Ross said nothing.

I said, "We've all been in a lot of situations and places we'd rather forget. This is one of those. Let's get back to the festive spirit."

Ross nodded. Jean wiped her eyes and tried a smile, a very small one, but a valiant try. Mary's glare dimmed.

I lifted my glass. "To the future and happiness for all."

Mary shook her head. "Ye gods, Tiny Tim!" But she raised her glass. Ross and Jean did, too, and they were both smiling.

The shadow of Talsman's visit hung over the court, though, and possibly the memory of George Ryerson. Some of the afternoon's sparkle was gone. We ate and talked and drank, but nobody laughed.

At five-thirty, Jean excused herself and Mary walked with her over to the apartment behind the restaurant.

Jack Ross looked at me thoughtfully. "What do you suppose gave Talsman the idea I had anything to do with the death of George Ryerson?"

"I don't know. Remember, he was drunk and irrational."

He nodded thoughtfully and looked toward the apartment. "It has certainly affected Jean."

"She's disturbed but I don't believe she's suspicious."

"Maybe. Maybe not. Are you finished with this job you were doing for Dora Diggert now?"

"So far as I know. I did what she hired me to do."

"How would you like to work a week or so on George Ryerson's murder?"

I shook my head. "The Department wouldn't stand still for a private man sticking his nose into a homicide. They'd pin my ears back good."

He smiled cynically. "Don't sit there and tell me you only work on cases the Los Angeles Police Department approves. I'm not that naive, Joe."

"I wouldn't try to tell you that, but murder is a long step outside the boundary of our tolerated investigations. And that's all the private man ever is, just barely tolerated."

"Your rates undoubtedly reflect the danger of that. What are your rates, Joe?"

"A hundred a day, plus the swindle sheet."

"I'll give you two hundred a day," he said evenly, "and a guaranteed minimum of a thousand dollars."

I thought a moment. "And if I get in a jam, am I permitted to reveal the name of my client?"

"Of course. I've nothing to hide."

"I shouldn't do it," I said, "even at that rate. But I will. I'll start tomorrow morning."

"Tomorrow's Sunday. Aren't you going to finish the weekend? We have room enough at the apartment."

"Thanks," I said, "but the weekend is already spoiled. Tom Talsman ruined it. I don't suppose you know who he's tied up with?"

He shook his head.

I said lightly, "And do you want to tell me why you're paying to have the death of George Ryerson investigated?"

"Because of Jean. I want you to investigate the possibility of my being involved, too. As objectively as though I weren't paying you."

I smiled at him. "I intended to do just that."

He laughed. "You are a man, Joe Puma." He beckoned to a waiter. "We'll drink on that."

"You're not so bad yourself," I told him.

The girls came back and I told Mary I planned on driving back to town tonight.

"I'm staying over," she said, "with Jean."

Jean looked quizzically at Jack Ross.

Ross said warmly, "An excellent idea! I wish Joe would stay, too."

I stood up. "I might as well start now. I'll keep in touch with you." I looked at Mary. "Shall I phone you, next week?"

She smiled. "Suit yourself. Is there any reason why you shouldn't phone me?"

"You're so—emotionally erratic, I didn't know if we were still friends."

She came over to kiss me. "We're friends. Thanks for everything."

I left them and went out across the flagstones to the gate and up the street to the motel. The manager told me it was rather late for check-out time, but since I was an old customer . . .

I told him, "You can check Miss Cefalu out, too. She'll be back for her clothes. She's staying with friends in town here tonight."

His face was blandly cynical. "All right, Joe. Did you find Ross? Is he the man you were looking for?"

"He's the man. If I get any calls from Los Angeles, you can tell the caller I'm on the way back there now."

I was packed and gassed and on the road west ten minutes after that.

The sun was low and in my eyes but soon the mountains blotted it and by the time I got to Riverside there was no glare, only the purple desert dusk.

Living as I had lived for a day and a half was bad for my morale. It helped to remind me how many ways there were to achieve that kind of living in my trade. One of the reasons I'd avoided marriage up to now was the certainty of the economic pressure it would bring.

The simple life was only appealing to simple people. Women weren't that; they were complicated and compelling creatures and they loved to force the top financial potential from a man. In my line, that road was easiest when one began to cut ethical corners and milk all shady angles.

Some of my contemporaries were doing very well supplying material to the filthy exposé magazines now enjoying a boom. They were selling out their clients. Others found blackmail a solid source of income.

I had cut a few corners in my time, but they were legal corners, not moral. Acquiring friends like Jack Ross could tempt me to further cuts.

Acquiring him as a client was much better for me ethically.

Riverside was still hot, but the air grew chillier as I came closer to Los Angeles. The stars were blanked out now by the overcast. I had a feeling tomorrow would be a smoggy day.

FIVE

THE MORNING dawned gray and overcast with a tinge of smog. Outside the door of my little apartment, the Sunday *Times* waited fat, pompous and patient. With my coffee, I read that the funeral of George Ryerson would take place tomorrow and there would be a number of prominent mourners. If there is anything the local papers love, it is prominent mourners.

I could assume the names had been clients of George's; I couldn't think of any other connection he could possibly have had with them. There were two famous cinema personalities, three TV lights and almost a dozen gentlemen listed as "sporting figures" or "restaurateurs." In our American language, this translated as hoodlums.

The mortuary was a house that often advertised "Complete Funerals From Seventy-Five Dollars" but I would bet a hundred to one that George Ryerson was not getting this blue-plate special. I decided the funeral would be a little too crowded for me.

I showered and shaved and phoned Dora Diggert.

"I suppose you think you're through?" she asked petulantly.

"I thought so. I found Jean and asked her to phone you. Has she?"

"She certainly has not."

"I asked her to. And she said she might. She said she had a few things she wanted to tell you. From her tone, I gathered they weren't things you'd be particularly happy to hear."

A silence, and then, "Is that Cefalu girl with her?"

"What made you think she is?"

"I've been trying to phone her and there's no answer.

She has a lot of influence with Jean and I humbled myself to the extent of trying to reach her."

"The Cefalu girl is with Miss Talsman," I said. "And also, I think Miss Talsman and Ross are going to be married."

"Married—?" Incredulity was in her voice.

"Why not?"

"He isn't the kind who marries. Believe me, I know."

"You know him well?" I asked innocently.

"Too well." Another pause. "Puma, I'd pay five hundred dollars to get Jean out of the clutches of that man."

"That would require some strong-arm stuff, Mrs. Diggert, and I don't handle that kind of assignment. Besides, I'm starting on another case today."

"I'll bet. Puma, for five hundred dollars to the right people, I could probably have Ross run out of the state."

"To the wrong people, you mean. Mrs. Diggert, you're mature enough to adjust to the inevitable, aren't you? Jean Talsman's found a home. That's always better than a house."

"I don't run a house, Dago. I run a service."

A horizontal escort service, I thought, but didn't voice. I waited for her to say good-bye.

Her phone said it with a sharp click.

The manager at the motel had made out separate bills. I enclosed my own in the expense statement I made out for the account of Dora Diggert. It had been an easy two hundred I'd earned and I considered paying my own expenses but that would have been bad business.

And where now? It was Sunday and the office of George Ryerson would not be open. It would probably be closed tomorrow, too, in memoriam.

I looked up Rafferty in the phone book and found an Eileen. The address was in the west end of town, so I didn't phone. I drove over.

It was a triplex of varnished redwood on National Boulevard near the Santa Monica Airport. Across the street, there was a new housing area and all the owners were out working on their sprouting lawns, or putting up new fences or planting shrubs.

The rear triplex was Eileen Rafferty's and her door chime was four-tone. She came to the door wearing polished cotton ivy league slacks and a shirt with a button-down collar. But nobody would be likely to confuse her with a boy.

Even in the gray morning overcast, her red hair glistened as she looked at me doubtfully and with no warmth.

"Puma," I said. "Joe. A private investigator, remember?"

She nodded. "I was about to start breakfast. What's on your mind?"

"George Ryerson," I told her. "I could run out and get some sweet rolls. Do you like sweet rolls?"

"I have some. Did you plan to eat with me?"

I smiled my warmest smile. "If you insist."

She seemed to be trying to read my mind. She made no move or no comment.

"I've been to Palm Springs," I said. "I found Jean Talsman."

"Why should that interest me?"

I shrugged. "I don't know. I was only making conversation. If you want me to leave, say the word."

She studied me. "Are you armed?"

"Not on Sunday morning."

"Well, I suppose you're harmless then." She opened the door wider. "Come in."

I came into a small living room furnished in Early American, touched with pewter and brass. A huge hooked rug covered the floor and a planter separated the dining alcove from this room. I sat in the dining alcove.

From the kitchenette, Eileen Rafferty asked, "Why are you interested in Mr. Ryerson's death?"

"Because the police seemed to think I was involved in it originally. In the event they return to that attitude, I'd like to give them somebody else to gnaw on."

She brought in a plate of sweet rolls and a percolator, which she set on the table. "How would I know anything about what happened to Mr. Ryerson?" She looked at me openly.

"I have to start somewhere," I explained. "There is always a possibility that you might have knowledge which you don't realize is important."

She poured my coffee and sat down across from me. She seemed to be thinking. Then she asked, "Did you read the *Times* this morning?"

I nodded.

"Did you see the names of some of the people who are attending the funeral?"

I nodded again.

"You're an investigator. You know the police records of some of those celebrities."

"I do. If any of them had a reason to dislike George, I can guess they'd be capable of resorting to the action that was finally taken. But I keep remembering that George grew agitated after my visit, that he broke that date for lunch after my visit. And he broke it undoubtedly because he had another date—with the killer."

"You can't be sure of that," she said.

"Doesn't he give reasons for breaking luncheon appointments?"

"Usually. Not that day." She paused. "Not to me, I mean."

"And he didn't tell you who he was meeting?"

She shook her head, her gaze meeting mine honestly. "And that's strange, because he usually does."

I asked her, "Did a man named Tom Talsman ever visit the office?"

She shook her head again.

I sipped my coffee. I had a strong feeling that she was lying to me but who could take a feeling into court?

The phone rang and she went to answer it. I heard her say, "I'm sorry; I have company. A Mr. Puma. I'll call you back." She hung up abruptly.

When she sat down at the table again, she seemed perturbed. I said, "Hope I didn't interrupt anything. A jealous boy friend?"

"Something like that," she said with a smile.

Again, I was certain she was lying.

I had no further questions for her; she had nothing to say to me. We sat in silence over our coffee. There was a definite possibility she could lead me to further knowledge, but I had no authority to get it out of her, and it seemed clear she wasn't going to volunteer anything helpful.

I finished my coffee and said, "It's a dangerous game, withholding information about a murder. It can easily lead to disaster. I suppose you know that?"

"I didn't," she said stiffly, "but I do now. Do you suspect me of withholding information?"

I nodded slowly and stood up. "Well, thanks for the coffee. And good luck, Miss Rafferty."

Her smile was cool. "Good luck to you, Mr. Puma. You can find your way out in a small place like this, can't you?"

"Easily," I answered, and went out into the gray Sunday with no further objective. I didn't want to bother Mrs. Ryerson today and there was no other person I could think of to visit. I should have stayed in Palm Springs.

The Bluffview shopping center wasn't too far from here; I drove over. The scene of the crime looked innocent enough this bleak day. It was ringed with small shops and all of them were closed.

Some of the shops were in two-story buildings; I went into all the lobbies that were open and read the lists of second floor business establishments.

Nothing rang a bell.

Why had the murder happened here? Motive, means and opportunity, that's the deadly triplicate necessary to all murders. Without motive, it's manslaughter. Without both of the other two, it doesn't happen. This hadn't been manslaughter, not a bullet through the temple. Motive—the word was trying to tell me something, something in the nature of a pun. It was swimming in the subconscious, trying to reach the surface. It didn't make it.

Was I wrong about manslaughter? Was it lack of motive that was trying to break through?

On the corner here, there was a branch of the Security-First National Bank. That seemed to be the only business in the center that could have anything to do with murder; an impressive number of homicides are committed for money.

I drove into Hollywood and had dinner at the Shorthorn. And after dinner, because it was close, I drove to the station on the off chance Sergeant Lehner would be around.

He wasn't, but a detective I knew by the name of Sands was there and he had some familiarity with the case. I asked him if Eileen Rafferty had been checked out.

He nodded. "Though only because of routine. She was in the office at the time Ryerson was killed. She took her lunch earlier."

"How about her background?"

He didn't answer that. He said, "Why are you interested, Joe? You're too smart to get involved in a homicide, aren't you?"

"Usually. Is Captain Jeswald in?"

"Not today. Friend of yours, isn't he?"

I nodded. "We went to college together."

"Uh-huh. Well, no police officer is enough of a friend to give you permission to stick your private nose into a murder, and you know that damned well, Joe."

"I've heard the rumor," I said mildly. "But I didn't think it applied to honest private men."

"No private operative is completely honest or he wouldn't be in business."

"If there wasn't a need for us, Sacramento wouldn't license us. I'll see Captain Jeswald tomorrow."

"Not if he sees you first. Be sensible, Joe."

Sure, sure. Credit reports and hotel skips, that's all they wanted to leave us. Stay out of the money cases, you licensed practitioners of private enterprise, stay out of the headline cases. You might build a rep. In a trade this high in occupational hazard, I should be able to go to Palm Springs at my own expense. More often. In Palm Springs, they would be laughing now, drinking good booze and eating fine food? Why had I come back to town?

My golf clubs were in the deck of the car and there was a sweater in the rear seat. I drove over to the Rancho Municipal Golf Course.

Rancho is jammed on Sunday, but I filled in with a threesome and teed off half an hour after I arrived. I finished thirteen holes before it turned too dark to play.

At home, I showered and settled down in front of the TV with a quart of beer to watch *What's My Line?* The commercial was on when my phone rang.

It was long distance and Mary's voice was happy. "We've been thinking about you."

"And drinking."

"Why not? What are you doing?"

"Watching television and sulking. And drinking beer."

"Beer? What's that? Jack has a rich friend who likes tall and skinny girls. Does that frighten you?"

"That's fine. Are you with him now?"

"Do you mean Jack?"

"No, I mean the rich friend. Is that why you're happy?"

"I'm not with the friend. I'm with Jack and Jean." A pause. "I miss you, Joe."

"I miss you, too," I answered. "Let me talk with Jack."

When he came on, I said, "I was down at the Hollywood Station this afternoon. An officer there told me I had better keep my nose out of this Ryerson murder. I planned to see Captain Jeswald about that tomorrow, but I thought you might be able to go even higher."

"I know somebody downtown," he said. "The Deputy Chief. Is that high enough? I can phone him today."

"That would be dandy," I said. "Let me talk with Mary again."

She came back and I said, "Take care of yourself, won't you? You know what liquor does to your—emotions."

"You're worried," she said. "How wonderful! How is it you never married, Puma?"

"I could never find a tall girl who was skinny enough or a skinny girl who was tall enough," I told her. "Now, you be good."

"Joe, darling, I will give it my Girl Scout best. But we don't want to get all tied up in promises, do we?"

"I guess not," I admitted.

"Don't sulk, Joe. I'm a big girl."

"Good luck," I said.

"Sweet dreams," she said, and hung up.

Women didn't need to be born rich. With any kind of passable equipment, they could always meet rich men. The only kind of rich women most men could get to were those over fifty who hadn't worn well. It was a woman's world.

I sat soddenly in front of the TV set, getting drowsy on beer. I watched Steve Allen. And hugged the small, warm knowledge that I was still better off than George Ryerson. At ten o'clock, I went to bed and slept the sleep of the poor and noble.

Monday morning dawned brighter than the previous day, though there was still some overcast. Captain Jeswald phoned me while I was attacking a bowl of corn flakes.

He said, "I understand you were looking for me yesterday."

"That's right, Captain. I wanted permission to help investigate the Ryerson murder."

"Who's your client?"

"Jack Ross. He owns a restaurant in Palm Springs."

"I know the man. Isn't his place where you found the girl you were looking for?"

"Correct," I agreed, startled. "You don't miss much, do you?"

"I try not to. Well, I've talked with the Chief this morning and we'll be tolerant with you. But make out a detailed report every day and supply us with a copy. Is that clear?"

"Yes."

"And another thing, Puma, you're working with us but not for us. You make that clear to everybody you interrogate."

"Check."

"And don't get muscular."

"Right."

He hung up and I went back to my corn flakes. This wasn't a police state we lived in, but that wasn't the Captain's fault. He would have welcomed one. At school, Jeswald and I had been fraternity brothers. He had no brothers any more; he was all cop.

The corn flakes were limp and the coffee bitter. It was last night's coffee. The *Times* had nothing new on the death of George Ryerson. The story was no longer front page news. There are too many homicides in this town and any big town to keep a murder important after the first couple of days. Unless the victim is headline-worthy. And the same new cases that come to the papers also come to the police department. No unsolved case is ever closed but the first few days see the maximum of investigation.

And how much work can be done after that first concentration of attention? The solution of a case after that initial effort is dependent on luck and the constant, twenty-four hour grinding of the general investigative machinery. A machine can only follow a pattern; there is no adjustment for the hunch, the whim, the calculated lie. Anything less than a machine would not be effective; anything more is not usually interested.

At my office, I checked the mail and my phone-answering service. There had been no calls and the mail was all third class.

It would be a morning funeral. I planned on seeing Mrs. Ryerson this afternoon. The morning yawned at me. I used an hour of it to type up in detail all the accomplishments on the disappearance of Jean Talsman. I added yesterday's labor to this on the assumption that the death of Ryerson was an extension of the original case. Until I proved myself wrong, that would be my approach. In the report, I tried to remember all the dialogue, even those words that seemed unimportant when voiced. Later, compared with other dialogues, they might somehow reveal a lie that could be turned into a lead.

It was ten-thirty when I finished, and I phoned Frank Perini, the gambler whose son I had found, the man who had recommended me to Dora Diggert. He wasn't home but his wife gave me a number where he could be reached and I caught him there. I asked him if he knew Jack Ross.

He said he did, and I asked him, "What's his reputation? He's never been mixed up with the Syndicate, has he?"

"Not to my knowledge, Joe. He's really a gambler only by inclination and not even that, these days, I hear. Inherited his money, you know."

"So I'd heard. He's never been heavy, then?"

"Hell, no! Have you ever met him? He looks like a cow college professor."

"Hoodlums can look like anything, Frank."

He chuckled. "Anything but Jack Ross. What's your beef with the man, Joe?"

"I have none. I'm working for him and I just wanted to make sure he was all right."

"God! I'm glad you're not working for me."

I thanked him again and hung up. Frank had been born in this area and had started gambling when he was seventeen. If Jack Ross had had any hoodlum tie-ups, Frank would have known about it and he would have told me. Of course, that still didn't mean Ross wasn't capable of murder. Only a small percentage of the homicides are committed by the organized hoodlums.

I ate lunch in Hollywood and phoned Mrs. Ryerson from the restaurant. I told her who I was and apologized for bothering her at a time like this. I told her I'd been hired to investigate the death of her husband and hoped she'd be able to see me this afternoon. She said she would see me at two o'clock. She sounded composed and calm and I remembered the story in the *Times* about her suit for divorce two months ago that she had withdrawn.

It was possible I was to meet another person who was not mourning George Ryerson. C.P.A.'s are likely to be insurance conscious; perhaps the widow had survived the calamity without undue grief.

At two o'clock, I pulled up in front of a two-story version of Hollywood Hills Norman architecture. As I turned off the ignition, the sun finally broke through the overcast and the well-kept lawn in front of the Ryerson home gleamed from recent watering.

To the south, I could see almost the entire city from this high vantage point. Thousands of cars were in sight along all the thoroughfares, but not a whisper of traffic noise penetrated to here.

A Negro maid answered my ring and told me Mrs. Ryerson was waiting for me in the living room. I followed her through a slate-floored entry hall to a long living room with beamed ceilings and leaded glass windows overlooking the city.

Mrs. Ryerson sat in a pull-up chair near the windows. She was a woman of medium height, getting faintly heavy, and there were no signs of mourning on her strong and attractive face. She could have been any age between thirty-five and forty-five.

She rose as I came in and walked over toward a davenport. Her figure was firm, if not slim. Her voice was low and a woman's voice: "Drink, Mr. Puma?"

I tried not to look surprised, but perhaps I did.

Because she added quickly, "I need one badly. It would look better to the maid if you drank, too."

"Whisky and water, thank you," I said.

"Bourbon?"

"Please."

"Would you mix them? I'll have the same."

She sat on the davenport as I went to the portable bar near the entrance to the dining room. I made her drink strong enough to loosen the tongue, hoping she was enough of a drinker not to gag at its potency. I brought both drinks back to the davenport and sat at the far end from her. She swallowed a good belt of the stuff and didn't even blink.

I said, "I've been hired by Jack Ross. Do you know him?"

She nodded. "There weren't many of my husband's clients I cared to have in my home, but Jack Ross was certainly always welcome."

Her voice was much more melodious than it had sounded over the phone. Her black hair was lustrous and thick; I was beginning to forget the middle-aged spread I had first noticed.

She said, "You're the detective who came to see George —that morning, aren't you? Wasn't it in the morning?"

"Around noon," I said.

She looked at me squarely. "About some girl, wasn't it?"

"Yes," I admitted. "Though I have since learned Mr. Ryerson had very little to do with the girl's disappearance. He simply acted as an agent for Mr. Ross."

She continued to look at me levelly and now she smiled. "Agent—? That's a polite word for it."

I said nothing.

"Let's be honest with each other," she suggested quietly. "George spent a lot of evenings away from home." She smiled meaningfully. "Have you met his receptionist?"

"Yes. But in the case I was working on at the time, your husband checked out as clean and uninvolved personally, Mrs. Ryerson. I have no other information on him."

"Maybe," she said, and held up her empty glass. "Would you mix me another?"

"Same strength?" I asked.

She nodded gravely. "Don't worry, Mr. Puma. I'm not going to be a problem."

It was hundred proof booze and I had put two ounces into her first drink. I mixed its twin and brought it back to her.

She looked musingly at the glass and asked, "What keeps a man away from home evenings when he isn't working?"

"Bowling, gambling, lodges, ball games, miniature golf. All the husbands who are out nights aren't necessarily chasing blondes, Mrs. Ryerson."

"True," she agreed. "But when they are evasive about where they have been, I think it would be fair to guess they weren't playing miniature golf, wouldn't you?"

"Maybe he was gambling," I offered. "He had a history of that, didn't he?"

"Not for years. And he wouldn't have to be evasive about gambling. I play bridge at ten cents a point, myself."

I sipped my drink. "Is that why you were going to divorce him a few months ago, because of some woman?"

She paused, looked at me carefully. "Have you heard any reason to the contrary?"

"Not yet. All I know about it was the mention I read in the newspapers."

She expelled her breath and said nothing.

I asked, "If I had nosed around, might I have heard something to the contrary?"

She looked at her drink. "You might have. George, like a number of unfaithful husbands, was pathologically jealous." She frowned. "Projection, I think it's called psychologically."

"He was jealous—and still went out every night?"

She nodded.

I said, "Would you be willing to give me the names of some of the women you suspect? Any investigation of them, naturally, would be extremely discreet."

"I haven't any names," she said wearily. "He was a very cautious man, George Ryerson. Except one name he mentioned a few times in his sleep. Mary."

"No last name?"

"No."

I said thoughtfully, "Actually, then, you can't be sure Mr. Ryerson was unfaithful, can you?"

Her chin lifted. "I certainly can. Perhaps another man wouldn't be as sure."

"Mrs. Ryerson, I didn't say that as a defense or as an argument. It's only that in an investigation of this kind, it is very important that we don't waste any time on hearsay or suspicion. It takes time enough simply to check out the facts."

She drank and said nothing.

I said, "Perhaps some of Mr. Ryerson's male friends would know about his—evening activities. Do you think I might find it profitable to question them?"

She shook her head. "The friends we shared, and those are the only ones you could believe, those friends are all above reproach. The others I don't even know."

"But those friends you shared might know about George's activities, even if they didn't share his moral attitudes."

"Not about George's," she said firmly. "He was careful; he was confident and he was cruel."

I had been right; this was another who wasn't mourning George Ryerson. We talked for a few minutes longer but I learned no more than I had in the first fruitless minutes. She had finished her second drink and was going to the liquor cabinet to mix another when I left.

In the entry hall, the Negro maid intercepted me. She stole a glance into the living room before opening the front door. Then she came out with me and closed the door behind her.

Her brown face was stiff with indignation and her low voice quivered with emotion. "I heard her. Running down that wonderful man, pretending to be the outraged wife. She makes me sick!"

I had finally found a mourner. I asked gently, "He was all right, was he?"

"To her, he was. The bills she ran up, and her from nothing. Do you know what she was—a floozie from Las Vegas, that's what she was, one of those girls walks around with the change for the suckers. And now she'll buy a four hundred dollar suit as though she never knew anything but Vassar and the good life. Such airs that woman can put on."

"How about the divorce?" I asked. "Was that her idea?"

The maid nodded vigorously. "And she still sees the man, too, one of those beach bums ten years younger than she is."

"Do you know his name?"

"It's right here," she said, and handed me a slip of paper. "I had it all ready for you. You look into him."

I promised her I would, and went down to the waiting Plymouth. Behind me, the Hollywood Norman house looked sedate and solid in the afternoon sun.

SIX

THE NAME on the slip of paper was Leslie Colt and the address was in Venice. He had to be an actor with a name like that; nobody was ever born Leslie Colt. With the last name, he was a cinch for westerns, and with the front name guaranteed box office in English drawing room comedies. How could he miss? One would expect he would be smooth and tall and taciturn, but the maid had said he was a beach bum. And who can stay smooth and tall and taciturn in Venice?

It is a beach town and was originally a delightful area, with its man-made canals and wide beach and sweeping view of the sea. But then oil had been discovered along its shores. So today Venice is a conglomeration of shacks and shabby homes, of oil pumps and raucous bars.

The address I'd been given was a four-car garage and for a moment I thought there had been a mistake. But then I saw some names on the stucco wall above the outside wooden staircase.

There were three names and numbers there and one of the names was Leslie Colt. I went up the steps to the open, railed runway that fronted on three doors. On the middle door, I turned the crank that rang a mechanical bell. I could see the beach from here.

The man who opened the door was not tall, about five-ten. He wore nothing but swimming trunks and his tanned body was almost grotesque with bunched muscle. His hair was sun-bleached, the face beneath it broad, attractive and pugnacious.

"Well?" he asked.

"My name is Joe Puma," I said. "I'm investigating the death of George Ryerson."

A flicker of annoyance in his bleached blue eyes. "So, who's stopping you?"

"Nobody, yet. You knew Mr. Ryerson, didn't you?"

"I met him once; I didn't know him. You a private eye?"

"I'm an investigator licensed by the state and currently working with the Los Angeles Police Department on this homicide. You can phone the Chief of Police if you doubt my authority."

He laughed. "Stow it! You'd be out of here in a hurry if I made a move to phone any law."

"If you have a phone," I said stiffly, "use it. I'll give you the number, if you want."

"Sure, sure. So all right, I met George Ryerson once. Any more questions?"

"You know his wife very well, don't you? His widow?"

He glared at me, his face tight. "What do you mean by very well?"

"Do you?"

"I know her. What's very well? You looking for trouble?"

"Any man," I explained patiently, "who looks for a murderer is automatically looking for trouble."

He smiled and his gaze traveled my length from top to bottom and back up. "How much do you weigh, Sherlock?"

"About two-twenty," I said. "The name is Puma."

He continued to smile. "Soft, too, I'll bet. Overweight, aren't you?"

"Stop racing your engine," I told him. "I came in peace, but no muscled beach freak ever frightened me and you'd be making a serious mistake if you tried to be the first. Don't you want to talk with me?"

His smile evaporated and he studied me speculatively. Then the smile returned. "Come in. If I didn't have a hangover, I'd try to be the first. It's your lucky day, Puma."

The room I came into held a studio couch and a kitchen table, a contour chair, three kitchen chairs and an ancient television set with a twelve inch screen. Cracked and peeling linoleum covered the floor. Beyond was a small kitchenette and an open door revealed a littered bathroom. It wasn't much compared with the home of the Widow Ryerson.

Colt asked, "Beer? I need one. Or do you tough eyes only drink rye?"

"Nothing, thank you," I said. "I've had my quota for the day. I guess Mrs. Ryerson didn't have the most faithful husband in the world, did she?"

From the kitchen, where he was punching holes into a can of beer, he looked out at me suspiciously. He shrugged.

"Did you ever meet Mr. Ryerson's receptionist?" I asked.

He frowned and shook his head. "Why?"

"Mrs. Ryerson mentioned her."

He tilted the can back and the muscles in his heavy throat moved as he gulped. He wiped his mouth with the back of his hand and came over to sit on one of the kitchen chairs.

Silence for a moment and then he grinned at me. "You don't think I killed him, do you?"

"I've no idea. Did you?"

He shook his head and tilted back in his chair. "Why in hell should I?"

"So you could move to Hollywood Hills," I guessed, "and get out of this miserable rattrap."

He stared at me thoughtfully. "I could have done that a couple of months ago. I'm the one who talked her into withdrawing the action. I'm not ready for marriage."

A thought came to me that I didn't voice. So many of these muscle men were, but those kind didn't break up marriages. I said, "I suppose you have a sound alibi for the time George Ryerson was killed?"

"I suppose," he said casually. "I'd have to think back. And I've had no reason to, yet. I'm not a suspect. You're really only looking for dirt, aren't you? Like all the rest of those private operatives the government is investigating right now."

"Believe me," I assured him, "you're as much of a suspect as any person I've met. You're the first with a motive."

He smiled wryly. "Okay, book me."

"I'm working with the Department, not for them," I explained. "I have no authority to bring you in."

"So," he said contemptuously, "we can sit here getting nowhere. Do you get paid for all this useless work?"

"It isn't always useless. You're not being very cooperative, Mr. Colt."

"I'm not getting paid to be. Look, Puma, I met a wife that wasn't being serviced and wanted to be. I filled the order. Can I help it if she gets some middle-aged romantic notions? I'm going to be a martyr?"

"You'd be a very well-fixed martyr, if martyr's the word."

"Well-fixed? Man, I know richer broads who are young, plenty of 'em. Why should I get chained to that biddy?"

I didn't answer. He went over to punch holes into another can of beer. Then he came back to recline on the contour chair, the only reasonably new piece of furniture in the place.

"Do you work, Mr. Colt?"

He chuckled. "Nights, I work. Get a real good stud fee, too. I'll bet you envy me."

"A little. But is that gentlemanly, to accept money for such a personal service?"

He yawned. "No money. They give me presents. They love to give me presents; that's half the kick in it for them."

"Either your fees are too low," I suggested, "or you aren't getting enough business. You should be able to afford a better apartment."

He smiled. "Nope. This is the right setting. They can look down on me. They can feel superior. I think they need to."

Blond and tanned and muscular, he relaxed in the contour chair, the all-American boy. Through the window beyond him, this clear day, I could see Catalina.

I asked, "Would you be this casual if I'd come up here with a Department badge? You can't be covered as well as you seem to think."

He yawned again. "Nobody with a badge has come up here yet. I'm supposed to worry about things that don't happen?"

"Nobody with a badge knows about you yet," I explained to him. "But you're going to be a prime suspect when they do."

He looked at me curiously. "Are you going to tell 'em about me?"

"I have to. I'm working with the police."

He stretched and smiled. "I'll bet. You're threatening me, Puma. But I'm not impressed. So long, big boy."

I stood up. "Then there's nothing about the death of George Ryerson you want to comment on?"

He nodded. "Yes. I wish he was still alive, so that chubby wife of his wouldn't be so hot about rushing me to the altar."

I left him without saying good-bye. I went out onto the railed runway and down the wooden steps. I was in my car and closing the door when I saw Tom Talsman.

He hadn't seen me. He was looking at the three names on the stucco wall. Then he went up the steps.

Now, there was a pair who deserved to meet each other, an arrogant duo destined to be soul mates. I got out of the car and went up the steps again quietly.

I stopped on the top step, around the corner from the runway, and heard Talsman say, "Don't get smart, blondie. I'm armed."

"Prove it," said Leslie Colt.

And then, a second later, I heard the thump and I looked around the corner to see Tom Talsman on the runway, blood dripping from one corner of his mouth. His .32 was also on the runway and Colt stooped to pick it up.

He emptied it, and as Talsman rose groggily to his feet, Colt handed it back to him. And said, "You're lucky. You caught me on a weak day. Now, if you're out of sight in five seconds, I might not even belt you again."

I went to the bottom of the steps to wait for him.

In a few seconds, he came slowly around the corner, holding carefully onto the guard rail with one hand, holding a handkerchief to his bleeding mouth with the other.

I said amiably, "This investigation game can be rough at times, can't it?"

He said nothing. He came to the bottom and stopped, to glare at me.

I asked, "Who gave you the lead to him?"

"None of your damned business," he said hoarsely.

"You're mistaken. It is my business. But not yours. You'll never be any good at it, Tom. Your attitude's wrong."

"Drop dead," he said harshly.

"What can you achieve?" I asked him. "You're going to wind up walking on your heels, the way you're operating. But maybe, if you tell me what you know, between us we can find a murderer."

"I know who you're working for," he said. "Get out of my way, Puma."

I stood to one side. "Talsman, I'm working with the Department, right now."

He went past me without another word. He climbed into a three-year-old Cad at the curb and gunned away. I drove to the nearest drugstore. From there, I phoned Captain Jeswald. I told him about Leslie Colt and Mrs. Ryerson and gave him the gist of my conversation with Colt. I added the Talsman epilogue and said, "Aren't you glad I'm on the case now? I'll bet this is all new to you, eh, Captain?"

"We'll bring Colt in," he said stiffly. "Keep us informed, Puma."

"Yes, brother." I said humbly. "Onward with Delta Kappa Epsilon."

"Don't give me that, Puma. You could have stayed with the Department, you know."

"I'll keep you informed," I promised, and hung up.

It was after four o'clock, now, and I was hungry. I phoned to see if Mary had returned from Palm Springs and she had.

"I'm hungry," I told her. "Have you got anything good to eat in the house?"

"One of those small canned hams and some beans. And a loaf of kosher rye bread. How does that sound?"

"Start opening the ham," I said.

Ten minutes later, when she opened her door to me, I could smell coffee and nail polish. I bent to kiss her and she gave me a cheek.

"Cool today," I commented.

"I don't want you to get any ideas," she explained. "I've a date for dinner."

I followed her to the dining area. She had made me two sandwiches. She went to the stove to get the beans as I sat down.

"Who is the date?" I asked. "The rich man who likes skinny girls?"

"No."

She brought me the beans and sat down across from me to pour herself a cup of coffee. She looked at me tenderly. "Isn't it strange what good friends we are? And a few days ago, we hadn't even met—"

"Nothing like a weekend in Palm Springs," I said, "to cement a friendship."

Her voice was low. "I wish you wouldn't be cynical."

I looked into her big brown eyes. "I apologize. When did you get back?"

"This morning. I drove in with Leonard."

"Leonard—?"

"The head waiter, you know—that glossy man who looks like a B picture heavy. I guess he comes into town often for Jack."

"Is he your date for dinner?"

She laughed quietly. "Oh, you are worried. We're not married, you know, Puma. We're not even engaged."

"No," I agreed. I sighed. "This is good ham." I ate some beans. "I saw Tom Talsman about an hour ago. I hope he isn't going to give Jean any more trouble."

Mary seemed to stiffen. "Is there any reason why he should?"

"I don't know. Do you know of any reason?"

She shook her head slowly. Then, suddenly, her eyes narrowed and she looked at me suspiciously. "Joe, are you —interrogating me? Is that why you came here today?"

"Of course not. I wanted to see you. But I have a feeling that even if you knew something that might help to solve a murder, you'd shut up about it rather than cause Jean any trouble. Is that correct?"

"That," she said calmly, "is probably correct. But I swear to you that I don't know anything about Jean that would help to solve a murder."

"You can't be sure," I argued. "You don't know what apparently innocent fact might be a key."

"All right, Puma, we're not going to fight again, are we?"

"No," I said wearily. "Mary, I'm working for that man you admire so much, that catch, Jack Ross. Fight him if you have to fight somebody."

She reached over to pour me a cup of coffee. I nodded my thanks.

"I'm sorry," she said softly.

"It's all right."

"No. I keep being suspicious of you and running down your profession and it's not right. Joe, that dinner date— it's purely business."

"You don't owe me any explanations."

Her voice sharpened. "Stop sulking, right now! Puma, you're a big, damned baby."

I laughed. "It's part of my charm. Now tell me about Jean."

"Believe me, Joe, there's absolutely nothing to tell. That's the gospel truth."

"Okay, tell me about Tulare, and why you have this phobia about being manhandled."

"Shut up," she said lightly.

I held my cup out. "More coffee, please?"

She poured me more and added some to her own cup. She looked past me at the gray day outside. "Why aren't we rich?"

"You could be," I said. "You could marry money. You could get almost any rich man you wanted and do him proud."

She shook her head. "You don't know them. They're cagey, unless you get them in college. And most of the ones I've met are so damned dull!"

"Why the blues?" I asked. "Because of Jean and her catch?"

"I suppose. That's envy, isn't it? And envy's petty."

"Petty and universal," I said. "Why don't we neck?"

"Oh, shut up. Tell me, who do you think killed Ryerson?"

"I haven't the beginning of an idea. But I'm sure that at least one person other than the killer knows and that gives me hope."

"Why are you sure of that?"

"I've been lied to so often. A clean case wouldn't bring forth this many lies."

She turned around to look at the clock on the kitchen wall.

"Don't rush me," I teased her. "I'm on the way."

She made a face. "You can stay and relax if you want. I have to take a shower and fix my hair and do a million little things."

I finished my coffee. "I'm going. Could we maybe see a movie or something this week?"

"I'd love it. Joe, be careful, take good care of yourself."

She came to the door with me and I kissed her on the forehead and thanked her for the meal. I went to the car feeling as I had all along; Mary knew more about Jean than she would reveal to me.

This whole thing had started with Jean and a highly involved date at a motel. Unless the time of Ryerson's death was an almost impossible coincidence, the fact of his death had to be connected with that motel date. That was the only logical sequence to examine and it was leading me nowhere.

And staying on the logic kick, Leslie Colt could seem like a logical suspect to the police, but I felt certain he would have no compulsion to kill Ryerson.

Unless he was a better actor than I imagined, he had no great lust for George's widow and no apparent motive beyond her inheritance. Logically, he wouldn't kill to get something he already had, the widow's body. And the money he could get through marrying her, he didn't intend to try for. He had had no motive for murder.

At least that was the impression his words and his attitude had left me with and I believed him for the moment. The police would learn if he had an alibi for the time; they would undoubtedly get more polite answers than I had.

The five o'clock traffic was jammed and tedious as I drove over to the office. There, I typed up the reports of the day and addressed one copy to Jeswald.

It was dark when I finished and the building was quiet. I took advantage of the quiet to once again review all the reports from my first and only interview with the deceased George Ryerson. Damn it, if these were the people involved in his death, a pattern should show somewhere. Nothing . . .

I phoned the Hollywood Station. Sergeant Lehner was there and I asked him if they had wormed anything out of Leslie Colt.

"Only some scandal," he answered. "We've got Mrs. Ryerson down here, too. Where'd you get this lead?"

"From an informant I'd rather not reveal. A true innocent, believe me, Sergeant."

"The guilt or innocence of an informant would be our decision, Puma."

"Not this time. What do you think of Colt as a suspect?"

"Not much, but he's the best we have, I'll admit. We're checking out his alibi right now. Listen, Puma, I want the name of that informant."

"That's too damned bad. You wouldn't even have the name of Leslie Colt if I hadn't given it to you. I can't work with any effectiveness unless you let me protect certain people. Now, we can argue this out in front of the Chief, or I can withdraw from the case. You have your choice of those two alternatives or the third one of permitting me certain freedoms. You decide; I don't like the case enough to make an issue of it."

Silence.

I said patiently, "I'm waiting, Sergeant."

"All right," he said angrily, "you win. Some day, Puma, I'm going to catch you with your pants down."

"Maybe." I hung up.

In my office, the desk lamp made a circle of light in the dark room. From the hallway, came a muffled, dragging sound and the hair seemed to bristle on the back of my neck.

I took my .38 from a desk drawer and went quietly to the door. The dragging sound was getting nearer and I jerked the door open quickly and stepped out into the hall, my gun ready and anxious.

The cleaning woman looked at me bewilderedly, the big pail on casters she'd been dragging rocked gently from her sudden stop. She looked at the gun in my hand and took a backward step.

"What's wrong, Mr. Puma?"

"Nothing," I said gently. "Nerves, I guess. I'm sorry."

She smiled. "It's a bad time. Miltown, that's what you need, Mr. Puma."

I went back into my office and slumped in the chair again. Where was the key to this tangle; where was the obvious lead? The word motive came back to haunt me, taunting me with its implied pun. Auto-motive—? That was part of it, but not the revealing whole.

That pail on casters had almost triggered the subconscious mind into spewing up the key I sought. Wheels, was that it? It certainly wasn't soap, detergent, mop, brush or broom. The mobility of the contraption had been the trigger. The casters had been the elusive suggestion to the key I was seeking.

I lived in a realist's world; the imagery and creativeness of my unconscious mind was atrophied from lack of use. Back in my realist's world, I went down to my workaday Plymouth and drove over to humdrum National Boulevard.

A quarter of a block from the triplex abode of Eileen Rafferty, I parked and waited. The stars were out and the night was clear. Lights glittered from all the picture windows in the housing tract and lighted planes took off from and descended on Santa Monica Airport. There had been a light, too, in the apartment of the redhead, though that didn't mean she was home. I had nowhere else to go; I waited.

I wondered if Mrs. Ryerson's grilling by the police would get to the newspapers. Not that I worried about her reputation, but the redhead had told me the widow had two children. It would be hard on them.

Down the block, a three-year-old Cadillac pulled to the curb in front of Eileen Rafferty's place. A man who looked like Tom Talsman got out on the street side and went up the walk to the rear unit.

In a few minutes he returned, and the lights from a passing car revealed to me that the man was, in truth, the ubiquitous Tom Talsman. In two minutes, this ineffective investigator had learned what I should have learned before I staked out.

Miss Rafferty was not home.

The lights of his Cad went swooping past as I ducked below the level of my windshield. When he was out of sight, I turned the Plymouth around and headed for home.

I was frustrated and unhappy as I pulled the Plymouth onto the vacant lot next to my apartment building. I was a fairly new tenant and all the garages had been occupied when I'd rented my apartment. I hadn't inquired since if there were any now vacant. I got out, and was locking the door on my side, when a voice from the dark said, "Welcome home, Puma. We've been waiting for you."

I turned to face two men. I couldn't see their faces clearly. Both of them were shorter than I but both of them also looked extremely broad.

"Business?" I asked, trying to keep my voice casual.

"Yeah. One grand. Just to keep your nose out of the Ryerson kill. It's worth a grand to us."

"I can't do that," I explained. "The Chief of Police has given me permission to work the case. He'll think it's mighty strange if I withdraw now."

"You don't have to announce you're quitting. Just get onto another line of investigation. A bum like you should know how to goof off."

I said, "I must be getting close to the killer, or you boys wouldn't be worried. Look, I'm working for a rich man. Maybe you could pick up a profit coming over to our side."

"Twelve hundred we'll give you. Fair enough, shamus?"

"I can't sell out," I said patiently. "This is my trade and I intend to stay in it. But you boys are just working for money; you'd be smart to string with me."

"Twelve hundred, Puma? This is your last chance."

"I'm sorry," I said.

The one on my right came in first, crowding me against

my car. I felt the door handle in my back and he hooked a left into my belly.

I lifted a knee and heard him grunt. I put my head down and felt the top of it crash his face. He started to curse and I found his throat with my right hand and tried to tear out his Adam's apple.

He gurgled out a choked scream—as the other man sapped me from the side.

Redness flooded my brain, but I was still conscious as I went down, conscious and powerless. As soon as I was prone, they began to kick me.

The last thing I heard, before a shoe caught my chin and brought oblivion, was the voice of the man whose throat I had held.

"God-damned snooping shamus," he was muttering.

SEVEN

OBLIVION is supposed to be black, but mine was red. There were undoubtedly many emotions contributing to my state of mind but the dominant emotion was hate. . . . I came to at the Georgia Receiving Hospital on a hard bed in a small room and looked into the sardonic face of Sergeant Lehner.

"Recognize either one of them?" he asked me.

"No. How do you know there were two?"

"One of your apartment tenants drove onto the lot as they were leaving. He got there a little late, huh?"

"I guess. How bad am I?"

"Three cracked ribs, a badly lacerated side. The doc isn't sure how serious the concussion is."

"How long have I been out?"

"Almost two hours. Is your headache bad?"

"Uh-huh. Did you get any kind of description?"

"Not much. What did they want, Puma?"

"They wanted me to get my nose out of the Ryerson murder. I tried to buy them over to our side."

"What made you think they were for sale?"

"Isn't everybody? Sergeant, I don't know who they were or who they were working for, if anybody. And I don't want to talk about them now. You know as much about them as I do."

"Why don't you want to talk about them?"

"It makes my headache worse."

"Puma, I hope you're not harboring any plans for personal vengeance on these two mugs. We don't work that way."

"Sergeant, I don't care a damned bit how you work. I am harboring plans for personal vengeance. Now run and get the nurse or doctor to give me something for this headache.

He inhaled heavily and held it. He glared at me. I closed my eyes. He expelled his breath and went for the nurse.

I slept without dreams and wakened to the smell of food. My headache was gone, but I had a strange, stiff soreness from my neck up and the attendant who brought my breakfast seemed to be surrounded by a red haze. After breakfast the doctor came in.

He smiled. "How do you feel?"

"Ready to go. Is that all right?"

"If you promise to take things easy for a couple of days."

"I promise. That is a lie, and you know it, but it relieves your responsibility, doesn't it?"

He nodded. "Cynical man, aren't you?"

He bent over to examine my ribs. He stood erectly after a minute, and said, "You may be released. But try to take it easy."

I promised him I would.

I hadn't been able to eat much of the hospital breakfast; I ate another in a restaurant in Hollywood. And went from there to the station. I had to walk carefully; any sudden jar made my brain rattle and my neck twinge.

Lehner wasn't at the station but the man working with him on the Ryerson case was. I asked him if any identification had been established on my assailants.

He shook his head. "Probably a pair of free lance muscle men for hire to anybody who has the price. It's a buyers' market for those, you know."

"I know. But in this case, the buyer could be the murderer. That makes them more important, doesn't it?"

He frowned. "Hell, yes. Who said they weren't important?"

"Your tone, your casual tone."

He studied me doubtfully. "I'm supposed to watch my tone? Puma, they didn't beat me up. I've got no personal beef with these slobs."

I said nothing.

He put a hand on my arm. "I'm sorry. But a word—don't go flexing your muscles. The Chief would pull you off this case fast if you did."

"I'm not bright," I explained. "I'm big, so my pride is physical. I owe this pair something and I mean to repay it."

"Don't," he warned me. "We've got the word to every stoolie in town that we want their names. Wait, and keep calm."

I didn't argue with him. The haze was dimmer now but still with me. I bought a paper and read it when I got to my office. The police had been kind; there was no mention of the fact that the Leslie Colt who had been picked up was Mrs. Ryerson's lover. He was identified as a friend of the deceased, and the story stated that he had been brought in for questioning, not for suspicion of murder. My own encounter was identified with the Ryerson murder and brought the murder back to the front page. There was a picture of me asleep in my hospital bed. I was reading this free publicity when the phone rang.

It was Mary. "I've been trying to get you ever since I saw the *Times*. Are you all right?"

"Up and around. I will be all right. Did you worry?"

"I've been frantic. Joe, you are going to rest aren't you?"

"Of course I am. As soon as I answer some letters, I'm going right home to bed."

"I've some appointments for today, but I could cancel them. Don't you want a nurse?"

"No," I told her. "I just want to lick my wounds in private. Don't be offended, Mary."

"Of course not. Now, you get home; don't bother with any letters."

"All right," I lied. "Okay."

I hung up, my head throbbing. I phoned a stoolie I knew and he told me he had already been approached, by the police. He said there wasn't a chance anybody would have a lead to the mugs. I told him I was paying a hundred dollars for any kind of lead.

From the next office came the sound of Dr. Graves' whirring, probing drill and it set my teeth on edge. I sat quietly in my chair, brooding. Outside, the overcast was heavy, the day damp and breezy.

In Palm Springs, my employer would be enjoying the sun with his bride-to-be, insulated from the violent, working world of Joe Puma by his money and his good sense. So, he hadn't twisted my arm; I'd taken this case of my own volition, motivated by my own love for money. I hadn't expected it to be easy.

My phone rang, and it was long distance from Palm Springs. It was the man I'd been thinking about. He said, "I've just read the *Times*. I didn't expect my hiring you would subject you to something like this."

"It's one of the hazards of the trade," I explained.

"Are you all right? The paper mentioned a concussion."

"I'm all right. Do you know Mrs. Ryerson well?"

"I've been to the house for dinner a few times. She's—" a pause, and his voice sounded embarrassed when he continued. "She's—well, would it be snobbish to say *socially ambitious?*"

"I guess not," I said. "This Colt you read about in the paper, if you did, was her lover."

"Oh—? Anything there?"

"I doubt it, or he wouldn't have been released. He must have given the police a satisfactory alibi. Is the sun out there?"

"Clear and hot. You and Mary must come out again this weekend. Only this time, you'll stay at our place."

I said, "I wouldn't want you to think I was socially ambitious, Mr. Ross."

His laugh was light. "Don't take any chances, Joe. Ryerson's death wasn't that important."

An unimportant death? Was there such a thing? Perhaps we had so much self pity in the world because it was the only kind of pity a man could expect. From the office of Dr. Graves came the sound of a child whimpering.

The blank wall of the Ryerson murder showed no holes. Last night had been the first move from the other side of the shadow and the men had gone back to the shadow, leaving no footprints.

I hauled out the typewriter and went on from where I had quit at six o'clock yesterday, trying to minutely record the short dialogue I'd had with my assailants before the action began. I also recorded the visit of Tom Talsman to Eileen Rafferty. My scene with the cleaning woman didn't seem significant, so I omitted that tableau.

It was past noon, now, but I wasn't hungry. I sat there, and my skin began to prickle. For no reason at all, I had a sense of something important impending.

The ring of the phone didn't surprise me in the least. I lifted it and said, "Joe Puma."

A voice said, "Had enough, monkey? You should be home in bed."

"I've been manhandled worse by higher-priced help," I assured him. "You boys are stupid; I'm on the money side."

"No kidding. Had enough?"

"Not yet. What kind of peanuts are you peons working for?"

"Enough." A pause. "Are you trying to buy something, shamus?"

I asked quietly, "Does twenty thousand dollars sound like money to you, shorty?"

"Huh! Who are you trying to kid? A cheap peeper like you—"

"My client's name is Jack Ross," I said evenly. "If you have any friends who move in better circles, you ask them about Jack Ross. And then call back at your leisure. It's just a question of time until we get the murderer, anyway. After that, you won't have anything to sell but your muscles again."

Another, longer pause, and then, "Twenty thousand—? Man, you're crazy—"

"Ten grand each," I said. "That's big money."

"There wouldn't need to be a split," he said thoughtfully. "My partner left town."

"Well," I said easily, "I won't keep you. Check around and phone back if you don't get a better offer." I paused. "And if you do get a better offer, there's a possibility we can match it. Check around, shorty."

"Don't call me shorty."

"You called me dago. Aren't you going to leave me anything?"

He laughed quietly. "You wouldn't consider yourself man enough to cross me, would you?"

"I've learned my lesson," I said humbly. "Phone me when you've learned yours."

"Will you be in your office?"

"For the next two hours," I answered. "And if the twenty grand doesn't appeal to you, maybe you could raise your offer to me and I'd consider dropping out."

"Twenty grand appeals to me," he said. "But what makes you think the person that hired me is the killer?"

"It's another step," I said. "All we're buying is steps."

"That don't add," he said suspiciously.

"Check around," I repeated. "I'm not going to argue with you, not after last night."

He hung up. I put the phone down and watched the sweat roll off my wrist. I sat very quietly, waiting for the redness to go away and for my heart to stop pounding.

I drank some cold water. I plugged in my electric shaver and shaved at my desk without a mirror, feeling for stubble. My face was wet and the shaver pulled and irritated.

He wouldn't phone back. He would suspect that I'd have a tap on my phone by that time and the police alerted to trace the call. He was undoubtedly a professional and no professional would use the phone after the initial call.

In the days before the unions had belatedly begun to clean house, men like my caller had been constantly and gainfully employed. Then, as they became respectable, the unions had been forced to clean the Commies and the thugs from their rosters. And these boys had been forced to free lance in order to stay in their trade.

Doc Graves came in to ask, "Going to lunch?"

"No. I want you to do something for me, Dale." I took out my checkbook and tore one check from it. "I want you to write out a check to me for twenty thousand dollars."

"Hell, yes," he said. "Glad to help out in any small way."

"I'm serious. And I want you to sign it Jack Ross."

He sighed. "All right. I won't ask why."

"Because the hoodlum might get suspicious if I made it out and then endorsed it in the same handwriting."

"Okay, Fosdick, give me a pen."

I gave him a pen and he did as I'd asked. He handed

me the check and asked, "Now, when this bounces, where do I send the ambulance for you?"

"Don't worry about me," I said. "Boy, you sure are hell on kids, aren't you? That one whimpering this morning almost tore my heart out."

"I'm painless," he said solemnly. "Any rumors you hear to the contrary are subversive."

He left, and I sat back again to wait. If my caller checked anyone in the know on Jack Ross, he would learn some facts that would substantiate my offer. He would learn about a man who had once bet fifty thousand dollars on the single cut of a deck, a man who had lost twice that in six hours of poker. I hoped he would ask the right people.

Two hours later, he hadn't phoned back. I strapped on the .38 and went out to the drugstore for lunch. From there, I went to the parking lot for my car.

And taped to the steering wheel with cellophane tape was a note for me. I read:

> Get right into the car and drive to 239 Gallo Way in Venice. We'll talk about the twenty grand there. Don't stop on the way.

I got right into the car, as the note directed. I pulled out of the lot and turned west on Olympic. Nobody followed me off the lot, but a block up, a Chev pulled away from the curb after I had gone past.

It was a common model, so I stalled enough to let him get closer. There was only the driver in the car, I then saw, and the last three digits of his license number were 079. The man behind the wheel seemed to be a wide man.

He followed me all the way to Santa Monica on Olympic, staying far enough behind so I wouldn't have noticed him if I hadn't been looking for him.

On Main Street, when I turned left off Pico, I watched the corner in my rear view mirror. He came around it when I was two blocks down Main.

In front of the Leslie Colt abode, a wino was tilting a bottle of muscatel to his mouth. He had the red halo and I wondered if that illusion was coming back. It could have been a reflection from a sign.

I turned left on Gallo Way and transferred my gun from

its shoulder holster to my jacket pocket before the other car came around the corner. Sweat trickled down my legs.

239 Gallo Way was a ramshackle cottage facing on the canal, with a sun-bleached picket fence and a front yard high with weeds. The sagging gate was ajar. Redwood chunks had been set into the ground for stepping stones leading to the narrow front porch.

I was on the porch when I heard the car pull into the back yard. The man in the Chev had evidently arrived by another street. I looked through the front window here and saw there was no furniture in the dusty living room.

Footsteps came along a wooden walk that skirted the side of the house and soon a pale man of medium height and impressive width came into view in the weed-filled yard.

He wore a dark suit and a blue shirt. His eyes were the same light blue as Leslie Colt's. His mouth was small and there was a thin scar running from his left ear to the center of his left cheek.

He came up onto the porch and smiled at me. "I followed you all the way from the parking lot."

"You're kidding! I'd have spotted you."

"Not me, you wouldn't." He looked me up and down. "Jesus, you are big, aren't you?"

I reached into my jacket pocket and brought out my wallet. I took the check from it and showed it to him. "My client sent that in this morning. Recognize the name?"

He nodded. "I checked it."

"With that kind of money," I said, "you can buy some furniture. You can fix this dump up."

"It's not mine," he said. "I'm renting it. Let's not gab out here on the porch." He went past me, a key in his hand.

Bile came into my mouth and the back of his head glowed redly. He opened the door and went in first. I followed him in, my wallet still in my hand.

The front door opened directly into the living room. It was a spring lock and it locked as it closed behind me. He turned to face me.

I still had my wallet in my hand. I put it casually into my jacket pocket and just as casually brought my .38 out.

He stared at the gun and at me. "Don't be a damned fool!"

"I won't if you won't. Believe me, I'm aching to kill you. You'd be foolish to give me an excuse. Take off your jacket."

He studied me for seconds. Then, carefully, he removed his jacket.

"Turn around," I said. "Drop the jacket on the floor."

He glared at me. "You think I'm crazy? You'll slug me."

"Better crazy than dead," I said. "I'll count to three."

"What can you gain?" he asked. "How can you win? You think I haven't got friends who'll get you for this?"

"One," I said. "Two—"

He turned around.

I caught him right behind the ear with the barrel of the .38 and he dropped like a sledged steer. The floor shook and dust danced in the air. I went into the kitchen and through it to a service porch. I found some clothesline on the service porch.

I came back in and rolled him over and tied his hands behind him. He started to moan as I was tying his feet together.

He had regained consciousness by the time I was finished. I grabbed a handful of his greasy hair and helped him to his feet.

"I've got a memory," he warned me.

I took him over to the wall and held him against it, my left hand firmly gripping his throat. I said, "Now tell me all you know about the Ryerson murder."

"You've gone nuts," he said. "You'll lose your license."

"I've gone partially nuts. Start talking."

"Go to hell," he said.

I put a right hand into his belly. Not with all my strength; I didn't mean to kill him. He grunted and cursed. I put two more in there and his pale face turned paler and this time he didn't curse.

"You're crazy," he said sickly. "You're not thinking."

I hit him harder. I took off his belt so I wouldn't skin my hand on the buckle. He was moaning now.

I held his throat with my right hand and hit him on the other side of the belly. He couldn't seem to get his breath. I waited.

"I don't know anything about Ryerson," he said, "so help me."

I hit him again and some vomit dribbled down over his chin.

"Honest to God, Puma, I don't! A guy named Talsman hired us, Tom Talsman." He opened his mouth wide, gasping for air. "God help me, that's the fact."

I drew my right hand back—and he started to cry.

"Where does Talsman live?" I asked.

"On Trader Street, in Santa Monica. His address is in my wallet."

I reached into a pocket and took out his wallet. I let go of his throat and he slumped to the floor, moaning quietly.

His driver's license was in the wallet; his name was Arno Eriksen. At least that was his current name. I went through the cards in his wallet until I came to one that held a Trader Street address. He nodded when I showed it to him.

I asked, "Want to tell me more now or should I go to work again? I'm enjoying this."

"So help me, Puma, that's all I know. It was only a job."

"What's your buddy's name?"

He shook his head stubbornly, sick as he was. I couldn't hit him for that. I had lied; I wasn't enjoying this. Nausea moved through me. Nothing was red any longer. If the man was really his buddy, I'd be meeting him soon enough. I went out, leaving the front door held open by a chair I brought from the kitchen.

From the first phone I got to, in a liquor store, I phoned the Venice Station. I said, "There's a very sick man who needs immediate medical treatment at 239 Gallo Way."

"Who's calling, please?" the officer asked.

"Leonard Stern of 245 Gallo Way," I said. "Would you hurry? The man has been attacked by somebody."

The sun was breaking through as I went out to my car. My stomach was growling and my conscience cringing. There was a persistent throb behind my eyeballs.

I started to get into my car and then thought of something else. I went back to the phone and dialed the Hollywood Station. I got Captain Jeswald and told him, "I've just learned that one of the men who manhandled me is named Arno Eriksen. He lives at 239 Gallo Way, in Venice. He was hired by a Tom Talsman, I learned."

"And where did you learn all this?"

"What difference does it make, Captain? Probably from one of the same stoolies who works for the Department. I'll keep you informed."

He growled something and hung up. As I went back to the car again, I could hear the wail of a siren getting louder from the north.

It was a short drive to Santa Monica, to Trader Street and the address I had found in Eriksen's wallet. It was an eight unit apartment building, with a pool. All the newer apartment buildings seemed to have pools. It was fieldstone, stucco and redwood, this building, and this certainly didn't appear to be a low rent district. Tom Talsman was either doing all right or not paying his rent.

His apartment was on the second floor and I went up an iron staircase to an iron runway that served the second floor units that faced on the pool.

I could hear the door chimes clearly but there was no response. I tried them again. Two apartments up the runway, a door opened and a heavy and heavily made-up woman came out, leading a cocker spaniel on a leash. They headed my way. When they were abreast of me, the cocker growled, straining at the leash, crying deep in his throat.

The woman said, "Stop it, Lester!" She looked at me. "He never does that."

The dog moaned and sniffed at the edges of the door. Then he backed away, whimpering.

The heavy woman's face was puzzled. "He must smell something strange, don't you think?"

"Definitely, ma'm," I agreed. "Which is the manager's apartment?"

The manager, she explained, didn't live here. A Mrs. Dural, in Apartment One, relayed any complaints or requests to the manager.

I went down to Apartment One and displayed the photostat of my license to a thin woman of about thirty wearing horn-rimmed glasses.

I said, "I suspect something might be wrong in Mr. Talsman's apartment. The way that tenant's cocker acted, I feel almost sure he smelled a dead man."

She gulped and looked at me anxiously. "I have a key— But don't you think it would be best to call the police?"

"Not yet," I answered. "Not until we're sure. C'mon, I'll go along with you. I'll go in first."

She came with me, bringing a ring of keys. In front of Talsman's door, she paused, and said weakly, "It doesn't seem right, somehow."

I took the key she held and opened the door. I stepped in and could smell nothing, but I didn't have a dog's olfactory sensitivity.

I didn't need it.

The thrice-humiliated Tom Talsman had suffered the final indignity. From the floor where he lay, his dead eyes stared at me as though I were a stranger.

I guessed I was a stranger to him now.

EIGHT

I WENT out to the runway again and said gently, "We'll use your phone. We don't want to disturb anything in here."

The thin woman put one hand on the wrought-iron railing. "Is he—Is Mr. Talsman—"

"We can't be sure," I lied. "The doctor will know."

This was Santa Monica. Hollywood is Los Angeles and so is Venice and Westwood, but Santa Monica is a municipality of its own, smug and snug and suspicious of outsiders who infringe on its apparent decorum. It is a town run completely from within and I didn't have a friend on the force. It is a tight town, rough on outsiders.

I wanted to leave, but I couldn't. A man was dead. I phoned the police and went out to the curb to wait for them. A patrol car came first. One uniformed man stayed with me; the other went up to Talsman's apartment.

My man asked, "You live here?"

"No." I showed him the photostat. "I came to see the man." I told him about the lady and the dog and my going down to get the key. I said, "I'm sure this is tied up with the murder of George Ryerson. I wish you would phone

Captain Jeswald at the Hollywood Station and tell him about this."

"So? You mean you've been working on that Ryerson murder?"

I nodded.

"A private investigator? Man, what won't they think of next in that town?"

"It's a big town," I explained. "They can't afford the coverage you boys can get in a little hamlet like this."

He looked at me resentfully. "Eighty thousand people? That's no hamlet." He nodded toward the apartment. "We'll wait up there."

Five minutes later, I was repeating my story to a detective-sergeant named Faust, a tall thin man with gray hair and tobacco-yellowed teeth. He didn't look like he was believing much of it.

When I had finished, he asked, "You say you're working with the Los Angeles Police Department? But for a client, no doubt?"

"Yes, Sergeant. A Mr. Jack Ross of Palm Springs."

"And what's his interest in Ryerson's murder?"

"I'm not sure."

He looked at me skeptically.

I protested, "The Los Angeles Department didn't think there was anything unusual about that."

He nodded contemptuously. "Puma, you're not in Los Angeles, now. You know that, don't you?"

"Of course, Sergeant."

He beckoned to one of the uniformed men. When the officer came over, Faust said, "Take this man down to Headquarters and hold him there until I come back."

"Wait—," I suggested. "Why don't you phone Captain Jeswald from here?"

He looked at me bleakly. "I'm busy. Is that all right with you, Puma?"

I didn't answer him. I went quietly, as the phrase goes.

At Headquarters, I sat with the uniformed man in a small room on the sunny side of the building. He didn't have any conversation to offer and there was nothing to look at in the room. I smoked and thought about Tom Talsman.

In a little less than half an hour, Sergeant Faust came

into the room. "All right," he said, "I phoned your Captain Jeswald."

"And?" I asked eagerly.

"And he's sending a man out for you. Something about an assault charge in Venice." He turned to the uniformed man. "Keep an eye on him."

My old fraternity brother, Captain Horace Jeswald, was fuming. He glared at me from behind his desk. "Who do you think you are? That man has internal hemorrhages. Who do you think you are—God?"

"I work for Him," I answered calmly. "What man are you talking about, Captain?"

"You know what man I'm talking about. Eriksen. Don't try to con me, Puma; he told us who assaulted him."

"I wouldn't ever call you a liar, Captain," I said, "but I will bet you ten dollars to ten cents that Arno Eriksen didn't tell any police officer that I assaulted him."

Jeswald half rose from his chair, his face livid.

"Cash bet," I added.

He said ominously, "Are you denying it?"

I nodded. "Take me to him. Let him make identification. I'm ready to go, right now."

He settled in his chair, steaming.

I reminded him quietly, "I give you Colt and Eriksen and Talsman. I don't turn around without informing you. And you're dying to throw me into the can on an assault charge. I've had it, Captain. I'm withdrawing from the case right now."

He took a deep breath. "You son-of-a-bitch— You and your fraudulent humility and your phoney sensitivity. As if I didn't know you. If you didn't bounce Eriksen around, who did?"

"I don't know, but I could guess. His partner."

"No kidding? And while you're guessing, could you guess why?"

I took out the twenty thousand dollar check and put it on his desk. I said, "I was ready to offer that to Eriksen and his buddy for the name of the man who hired them. I figured them for hired help. Eriksen told me there wasn't any reason to split; his partner was out of town. The way it turned out, I guess his partner didn't stay out of town."

Jeswald leaned back and lighted his pipe. "Keep talking."

I took out the note that had been taped to my steering wheel and put it on his desk next to the check. "I found this in my car and went out to Venice. The door was open and Eriksen tied up in the house. He told me to get to Talsman in a hurry, and that's exactly what I did."

"You could have untied him in the time it took to make that phoney call to the Venice Station and the call to me."

"I didn't think untying him was as important to his health as getting medical help there in a hurry."

He puffed on his pipe and read the note. He looked up and said, "I hope you don't think I believe a damned word of all this nonsense?"

"Take me to Eriksen," I said calmly. "Let him make identification and then you can book me. I've told you my story."

He said nothing, staring uncomfortably at the note and the check. Finally, he handed them both back to me. "You were correct about Eriksen; he didn't name you. But he'll be out of the hospital one of these days and his partner is still around. Perhaps they'll do the job on you we can't."

I stared at him. "Would you be happy to see that?"

He rubbed the back of his neck. "No, no, of course not. It's been a bad day. Get out of here."

I stood up. "Eriksen is scum, remember that. You're confusing him with a citizen."

He looked at me unwaveringly. "At the moment, I'm running down a rumor that this Jean Talsman was a call girl. She and her roommate are going to be thoroughly investigated. I don't believe the roommate ever hired you."

"Think what you must," I said, "and then balance it against the knowledge that I gave you Colt and Eriksen and led you to the body of Talsman. Judge me completely, when you start, Captain."

"Beat it," he said.

"I'm an ally," I went on. "I'm an ally and a damned valuable one."

He looked at his pipe and he looked at his desk and he finally looked at me. "Okay, okay, you could be right. Now will you beat it?"

I winked at him. "Sure thing. See you around—brother."

I left him with his pipe and his conscience and went out into the rush-hour traffic of Hollywood. Carbon monoxide from a million belching tail-pipes poured smog into the Los Angeles Basin. My eyes smarted as I looked out at the yellow pall highlighted by the setting sun. The corn-belt refugees who complained about it the most were the people who were actually responsible for it. This area was growing too fast.

I went back to my office, which was in another separate municipality, the millionaire's haven called Beverly Hills. There, I tore up the bogus check and filed Eriksen's note. Then I typed the story of my adventure since last I sat at this desk. The bit about Eriksen at the house in Venice I fictionalized, as a copy of this report would be going to Captain Jeswald.

I took two aspirin and sat by the window, watching the sun go down and the traffic dwindle. I was ashamed of my part in that Venice violence; I tried to rationalize it away by telling myself I hadn't been mentally sound since leaving the hospital. But though I could lie to others with fair success, I had never properly learned to lie to myself with conviction.

Below my window now, an Imperial was pulling to the curb in front of the building entrance. A man of about sixty got out on the curb side; a heavier, younger man got out from behind the wheel on the street side. I thought I recognized the older man; I went back to my desk.

I heard their footsteps on the stairs and coming down the hall. I pretended to be absorbed in my reports, though my .38 was in a handy desk drawer and the drawer was open.

It says "Enter" on the frosted glass of my office door and that's what they did. I looked up and stared at the older man.

"Joseph Puma?" he asked.

"Yes. And you're Dennis Greene."

The other man lifted his eyebrows. Greene's face showed nothing. He asked mildly, "How did you know?"

"I saw you when you appeared in front of the Kefauver Committee."

He winced wryly. "Ouch! Absurd farce, wasn't it?"

The other man smiled. I said nothing.

"We came," Greene said, "to inquire about a man named Arno Eriksen."

"He's in the hospital. You could check there."

"We've already been there. You're not very gracious, Mr. Puma."

"I don't like crooks," I said.

The younger man stiffened; Greene remained calm. Greene asked, "Would you answer some questions for us?"

"Ask them, and I'll decide."

The younger man growled something and Greene turned to him. "Wait in the car."

The man started to protest, hesitated, and then turned and went out.

"Eriksen's partner?" I asked.

Greene glanced toward the door. "Him? No! What made you think he might be?"

"Just a random guess. Sit down, Mr. Greene."

He came over to sit in my customer's chair. He settled himself comfortably and said, "Arno Eriksen has worked for me from time to time. I haven't had any need for his rather narrow talents recently, but I retain a sentimental interest in his welfare and try to find him work when I can. I thought perhaps his trouble with you might concern me."

"It might," I said. "He and his partner offered me twelve hundred dollars to stop investigating the Ryerson murder. When I refused, they put me into the hospital. When I came out, Eriksen approached me again and I offered to buy some information from him." I leaned back. "And he fell for it."

"And you beat him up?"

"I don't remember. You're Mr. Eriksen's employer, are you?"

He shook his head, looking at me thoughtfully. "Not exactly, and certainly not on this bit of violence. Mr. Puma, believe me, I had nothing to do with your misfortune or the Ryerson murder."

"Okay. I'll believe you if you tell me the name of Eriksen's partner."

"You know I can't do that. I want you to know they were free lancing and that murder is never any part of my operations."

"Unless it's necessary," I added. "Are you going to keep that pair from bothering me again?"

"I can assure you they'll not trouble you again."

I smiled. "In writing, Mr. Greene?"

He frowned. "You're being unreasonable. Or was that an attempt at humor."

"I'm afraid it was," I admitted. "Well, there's nothing else?"

"Only one question and I know most private investigators resent it—but would you want to tell me the name of your client?"

"Jack Ross," I said. "He lives in Palm Springs."

"Ah, yes . . . I know Jack very well. Give him my best, won't you, when you see him?"

"I'm not sure your best would be good enough," I said, "but I'll forward it."

For an unmasked moment, he must have forgotten his advanced age and current respectability. Because he said hoarsely, "Some of your humor, Puma, borders on insolence."

"All the better humor is based on disrespect," I explained to him. "You're a rich man today, Mr. Greene, and probably admired in a number of pseudo-respectable circles. But too many widows have reason to remember what you really are. And now, if you don't mind, I'd like to get back to work."

He went out without answering and I did what I should have done two hours ago. I phoned Palm Springs.

Jack Ross wasn't there; I talked with Leonard. I told him, "I should have phoned earlier, but I've been kept busy. Does Jack know Jean's brother was murdered?"

"He does, Mr. Puma. They left for Los Angeles an hour ago."

"I see. Leonard, do you know Dennis Greene?"

"I guess everyone knows him, Mr. Puma. Why do you ask?"

"He claimed to be a good friend of Jack's. It was a pair of Greene's hoodlums who clobbered me yesterday."

"Mr. Greene was never a good friend of Mr. Ross's. You can be sure of that, Mr. Puma. Mr. Greene is a name-dropper."

I hung up and added Greene's visit to my report of the

day. When he had appeared before the Kefauver Committee, some newspaper wag had labeled Greene "Dennis the Menace" and that had reputedly been a bigger blow to his ego than being summoned by the Committee. He certainly acted like a man who took himself seriously.

I phoned the Hollywood Station and was told Captain Jeswald had gone home. I phoned him at home and told him about Greene's visit.

"I'll have him brought in in the morning," he said wearily. "Tonight, I'm going to rest."

"Captain, I think we're finally getting somewhere. The creatures are beginninng to crawl out of the woodwork. Somebody will break."

"Maybe," he said. "Maybe. Good night."

"One second, Captain. How about Talsman? What killed him?"

"An ice pick. The temple, again. Though I just a few minutes ago got a report from Santa Monica that he'd been fed chloral hydrate, too. In alcohol. Which should mean he had been drinking there in the apartment with somebody."

"Chloral hydrate wouldn't kill him, would it?"

"Combined with an ice pick, cream puffs will kill you. He died about eleven o'clock last night. Where were you at eleven o'clock last night, Puma?"

"In the hospital, remember?"

"Well, that should clear you. Where was your client at that time?"

"In Palm Springs, no doubt. I won't keep you any longer, Captain."

A pause. Then, "Good night. Working late, aren't you?"

I thought of a nasty crack in answer, but didn't voice it. He'd had a bad day.

I phoned Mary and told her Jack and Jean were on the way to town and asked her if Jean had phoned.

"Yes. They're going to stay here. Why don't you come over for dinner? They'll be here by eight and we'll eat then."

"Maybe Jean wouldn't want company."

"I think she would. Could you pick up some steaks? I'll pay you for them when you get here."

"Sure, sure. And you think I should come?"

"I certainly do. I want to look at you, Puma. I like your looks."

Those had been the kindest words I'd heard today. I hung up gratefully and went down to the washroom to wash my face and brush my teeth.

It had been a hectic day, climaxed by the violence in Santa Monica. That murder was Santa Monica's and though I was certain it was tied up with Ryerson's death, it seemed likely I would have trouble getting any information out of the bay city Department.

Trouble, hell; without the intervention of some powerful friend, it would be impossible. Even the Los Angeles Department would have trouble getting information out of Santa Monica.

Well, Jack Ross would probably know somebody . . .

The steaks I bought were filets and I wouldn't accept Mary's money for them. As I explained to her, we had eaten the finest and guzzled the best in Palm Springs. This was a small payment on that.

"And he wants us back," I said. "We've got a wealthy friend."

"Maybe," Mary mused, "he could give you a good job and you could afford a wife."

"I can afford an inexpensive wife, right now."

"That isn't the kind you'd want. Do you know how to make a decent Martini? With some vermouth in it. I don't mean one of those tinted gin things."

"Yes'm," I said. "Tom Talsman was killed with an ice pick. Does Jean know that?"

"I've no idea and I'm certainly not going to ask her. The paper said something about his being drugged, too."

"What paper? I didn't see anything in the papers about that."

"The *Santa Monica Outlook,* natch. For local news you have to read a local paper." She nodded toward the living room. "It's on the coffee table in there."

I put the Martini glasses in the freezer section of the refrigerator and went into the living room to read the *Santa Monica Outlook.*

There was very little there I didn't know. There was, however, one paragraph that was news to me. I read:

> Mrs. Castle, a new tenant in the building, has the apartment next to Talsman's. She stated that between ten and eleven o'clock she heard some murmuring in the next apartment and then heard one shouted lewd remark and the talking ceased. The police have refused to reveal the shouted words but it might be significant that an immediate roundup of the known deviates who patronize the pier section known, to our local shame, as "Queer's Alley" got underway immediately after Mrs. Castle's statement.

From the kitchen, Mary asked, "How about that bit regarding our local shame. I don't think its existence would ever be publicly admitted.

"I thought all the lavender lads hung out in the Santa Monica Canyon."

"Some do, not all. Tom didn't seem like—one of *those,* did he? You had better hide that paper. I don't want Jean to see it."

I brought the paper out to the kitchen and she put it in the wastepaper basket. I suggested, "Maybe Tom did the shouting. Maybe it was his visitor who was queer."

"Wouldn't the paper say that Tom did the shouting?"

"It doesn't state he didn't. And a new tenant might not know Tom's voice. You know, this brings me back to Leslie Colt. A lot of those muscle men are double-gaited. And he certainly lived close enough to that house on Gallo where I met Eriksen. This Colt was released too soon."

"Take it easy," Mary advised me. "You don't even know what the remark was. And you don't know who shouted it, Tom or his visitor." She smiled and patted my cheek.

"Why should I take it easy? Are you afraid I can't handle Leslie Colt?"

"I don't want you to go off half-cocked. Your Latin temperament gives you a tendency to go charging in without thinking things through first."

I asked quietly, "Do you know anything about Tom Talsman that I don't?"

"Don't look at me like that. No, I don't."

I leaned against the refrigerator and watched her make the salad dressing. Her hand trembled as she poured the oil.

"You're nervous," I said.

She stared at me. "Ye gods! Jean's my best friend and she'll be here in an hour. And her brother was just killed. I simply don't know what to say or do."

"Oh."

She continued to stare at me. "Puma you're not playing Dick Tracy at the moment, are you? Not now?"

I shook my head.

"If I really thought you were," she said, "you'd be wearing this salad dressing."

"Your Latin temperament is getting the best of you," I said calmly. "Couldn't I have a sandwich or something? I can't wait until eight o'clock to eat. I'll get sick."

"There's some of that canned ham left. Make your own."

I made a ham sandwich and warmed the left-over coffee. I ate in the dining area in a chair that faced the kitchen. I liked to watch Mary move. I like to watch any attractive and poised female move. They make an art of it.

If Tom Talsman had been killed by the same person who killed George Ryerson, Tom's death should help to delineate a path to the killer. The path was no clearer to me. The perversion angle opened new lines of investigation, but they might be confined to Santa Monica. Where I had no influential friends.

I sipped my coffee. Mary stood with her back to me, facing the sink. I saw her shoulders tremble and I got up immediately and went over swiftly to put my arms around her. She began to cry.

"Everybody dies," I told her. "Everybody."

She dried her eyes and kissed me. "I'll be all right." She put her long, slim fingers to my lips.

She was drying her eyes again when the door chime sounded. Three seconds later, she was crying once more, as Jean and she held each other and sobbed.

Jack Ross looked at me uncomfortably and I returned the gaze with the same discomfort. He went to the kitchen, and I followed.

In the kitchen, he poured a stiff jolt of whisky and drained it in one gulp. He expelled his breath and looked at me. "I've a feeling Jean is leary about me." He poured another drink. "I came to town last night, you see. It was a poker game."

"You drove all that distance for a poker game?"

His eyebrows lifted. "Why not? Jean wasn't feeling well and she wanted to go to bed early. And this was a gang I love to tangle with." He sipped his second drink. "A game every three months; is that too much, Joe?"

"It's unfortunate it was last night. Captain Jeswald asked me a few hours ago where you were last night."

"Well, I'll have all the witnesses to that I'll need. And I'm sure they're solid enough to impress your Captain Jeswald, whoever he is."

"Do you know Dennis Greene?"

He smiled wryly. "Dennis the Menace? Everyone knows him, that lavender lovely."

"He's queer— ?"

Ross shrugged. "Who knows? Who can ever be positive? He never married and the nasty rumors about him have remained constant for a number of years."

"You never married," I said.

He looked at me thoughtfully. "Nor you. Shall we dance?"

"Greene claimed to be a good friend of yours when he came to see me. He asked me to send you his best."

"He's no friend of mine. Joe, what are you driving at?"

"Homosexuality has reared its repulsive head." I told him about the account in the *Outlook* and asked him if he knew any police officer in Santa Monica.

"No, but I know a reporter on the paper there." He went to get the phone book. He found the reporter at home and asked him if he knew what the shouted remark was. He had the man repeat it for my benefit. The remark was: "—you stinking homo, I know what you're planning—"

I asked the reporter, "Was that said to Talsman? Or did Talsman say it?"

"Nobody knows. A few of the local fags claim to have known Talsman well, but what does that prove? Some of my best friends are fags. And I've got five kids."

When I hung up, Jack Ross was staring out into the dining area, lost in thought.

I said, "Jean will snap out of it. She really couldn't have loved him so much, or she would have seen him oftener."

He nodded, but he didn't look hopeful.

NINE

JEAN stayed with Mary in the bedroom while Jack and I broiled the steaks and mashed the potatoes and made the coffee and heated the rolls. It was a quiet, gloomy meal and Jean scarcely touched her food. Nobody seemed to have anything to talk about. I was almost sorry I had come. After dinner, Jean and Jack left to make arrangements with a mortician and I helped Mary with the dishes. She was in a blue funk.

I told her, "When a man decides to get into the rackets, he knows there's a strong possibility he will die a violent death. With anyone as belligerent as Tom Talsman it could happen early."

"I'm not thinking of him. I'm thinking of Jean."

"They weren't so close, were they?"

"As kids, they were very close. It was a great disappointment to Jean when she learned Tom was involved with hoodlums."

"So she made up for it by leading a blameless life?"

Mary said tightly, "Easy, Puma. You're on thin ice."

"I'm asking you to be reasonable. If that puts me on thin ice, so be it. Your morals are a little confused, though, sister."

"Go," she said. "Leave."

"Relax," I told her.

She looked up and her eyes were agates. "I asked you to leave. Do I have to call the police to get you to leave?"

I put down the dish towel and reached out for her. She backed away, water from her wet hands dripping on the kitchen floor.

"Damn you, Joe, don't touch me! I've had enough of you this evening. I want you to go right now."

It wasn't a time to argue. Nor, I felt, was it a time to leave her alone. I went out and sat in the Plymouth in front of her apartment. When Jack and Jean returned from the mortician, I left. There were a few places I could have gone and perhaps should have gone but I was tired and spiritless. I went home.

I stayed in the shower a long time, letting the stiff, warm spray massage the back of my neck and my taut shoulder muscles. Then I came out with a robe on and sat down with a can of beer to wait for the eleven o'clock news report on Channel Four. The commentator gave a little more than a minute of his time to the death of Tom Talsman and made no mention of the shouted lewdness. I finished the beer and went to bed.

The morning *Times* had a front page story on the Senate Interim Committee currently probing the private investigation racketeers in this area. The piece about Tom Talsman flanked this story and my name was prominently mentioned.

I had been damned by make-up proximity. A certain amount of unfavorable publicity is good for a private investigator's business; we don't get clients who would be better served by the police department. But connecting an investigator with any kind of Congressional committee was the road to bankruptcy in these frightened 'fifties.

Perhaps Mary was right. Perhaps I should butter up my rich friend, Jack Ross, in the hope that he would make a place for me in his operations.

Motive, motive, automotive . . . I was trying to digest this with my Wheaties when the phone rang.

Mary said, "I'm sorry, Joe. I haven't time to talk, but I had to take the time to tell you I was sorry."

"Thanks for calling. You're a sweet, warm, loyal girl and it would be a wonderful world if everybody was like you."

"If everybody was like me," she protested, "there wouldn't be any men. And that would be a horrible world."

"Not for me. Take care of yourself. I'll phone you later."

Motive, motive, automotive . . . People always phoned me right after I had put the milk on my breakfast cereal and I always came back to a limp dish. Motive, motive, automotive . . . To hell with that. I read that Arno Eriksen was still in the hospital, though his condition was hearteningly improved. No success had been achieved in the search for his assailant.

What search? The newspapers hadn't even been informed that Arno was one of the boys who had clobbered me. The only search, if any, being made for his assailant would be made by his partner. I hoped that Arno's side-kick was still out of town and that they were not really close friends. Hoodlums aren't likely to be out-foxed twice and there would be no financial complications limiting their next visit. They would be out for something simple, like revenge.

My headache was gone but my ribs were still sore. I washed my few dishes and shaved and went to the office. The mail consisted of one bill, no checks. A throwaway shoppers' newspaper and two car dealers' ads claiming to have many models priced below the "so-called low-priced three."

It was another overcast day and I was at a dead end. A brighter man might have glimpsed the pattern by now; I sensed that the solution was about to bite me on the nose. Frustration and a feeling of insufficiency gnawed at me. The day's dullness didn't help. Well, the Department wasn't being any more successful and they had thousands of men and acres of equipment. I had helped them more than they had helped me. Carry on, Puma, win, lose or draw.

I phoned the office of George Ryerson and Eileen Rafferty answered. I asked her, "Would it be possible for you to have lunch with me today?"

"Why should I? I've already been interrogated by the police."

"About what?"

"About my—supposed relations with Mr. Ryerson. His widow has a nasty mind."

"George might have given her reason to have a nasty mind. He wasn't exactly a saint, you know."

"And I'm not exactly an adulteress, Mr. Puma. I see no point in having lunch with you."

"I'm single," I argued, "and you could pick an expensive place to eat. What can you lose?"

A pause. And then her voice became warmer. "All right. I'll meet you at Stormoff's at one o'clock.

I replaced the phone and turned around in my chair to stare out at the sullen day. I thought of all the people I had questioned and had heard from and about, looking for relationships.

Finally, I took a piece of typing paper and printed each name in a separate box on it. Then, with lines, I connected the names that had obvious connections, such as Jean and Mary and Ross. I connected Greene with the hoodlums tentatively and the hoodlums with Talsman definitely. I put a tentative line between Eileen Rafferty and George Ryerson. I made the tentative lines light and the obvious relationships darker.

I was getting nowhere, but having fun, when Sergeant Lehner walked in. He seemed unhappy.

"Welcome," I said. "I was about to make some coffee. Would you like a cup?" I went over to put the water on my hot plate.

He slumped down in my customer's chair. "I thought it was about time we had an honest meeting of minds, Puma." He paused. "And exchange of information."

"*You* thought? Or your superior thought?"

He said evenly, "I'd like to talk without any of your sarcastic humor. Will that be possible?"

I nodded, and turned the plate to high. I came back to sit behind my desk. "What did you boys learn when you questioned Eileen Rafferty?"

"Not much. Except that it seems Mrs. Ryerson was pathologically jealous."

"Even though she was back-dooring Ryerson?"

He nodded. "Those are the kind, I heard, who are the most jealous. The psychologists have a name for it."

"Projection," I supplied. "It's a word Mrs. Ryerson gave me when she was explaining about George. He was jealous, too. How clear is she for the time her husband was killed?"

"Solid. The maid supports her and the maid isn't exactly in her fan club. I suppose that's where you got the lead to Colt, from the maid?"

"I suppose. How about this homo angle on Talsman?"

"If we picked up all the homos in this area, we'd have to fence off Griffith Park to hold them. It could tie Dennis Greene in, though. Did he threaten you yesterday?"

"No. He accused me of insolence. Otherwise, it was a friendly visit."

Lehner rubbed his temples. "I thought you saved your insolence for us. Isn't that water boiling yet?"

"Not yet, Sergeant. You know, if that other hoodlum

thinks there's a dollar in this business, he'll be back to see me. And Eriksen, too, once he's out of the hospital."

He smiled dryly. "Even if there isn't a dollar in this mess, either or both could be back because of the job you did on Eriksen. That's what you're really thinking."

I looked at him innocently. "Didn't Captain Jeswald explain that to you? I wasn't the one who beat up Eriksen. Don't you read the papers, Sergeant?"

He yawned. "Stop the bull, Puma. I'm glad I'm not you right now."

"The Department will protect me," I said. "I have a lot of faith in the Department. That water's hot enough now."

I took out two cups from a drawer of my desk and put some instant coffee into them. I poured the hot water and said, "No cream or sugar. Sorry."

He leaned back and sipped the coffee. "Cozy, aren't you? What do you charge the suckers, Puma?"

"A hundred a day."

"Man, that's thirty-six thousand a year, if you work every day."

"It's about nine thousand a year, net," I said. "My best year was fourteen thousand. And that was because of bonuses for exceptional service. On my daily rate, I wouldn't come near it."

"It's a lot more than I make," he said.

"You could get a license and try it, Sergeant."

He said nothing. He rubbed the back of his neck and looked gloomily past me, out the window.

"You're nowhere in this case, aren't you?" I asked. "Just like I am."

His glance came back to meet mine. He didn't speak. I returned the favor.

Finally, he said, "That Jean Talsman is a call girl, isn't she?"

I hesitated between loyalty to Jean and the necessity of my staying in business. Thoughtfully, I said, "I'm beginning to think she was. Not any more, though. She's marrying money."

"Ross?"

I nodded.

"He's clear enough, on Talsman. One of the men he played poker with is in the D.A.'s office."

"He's respectable," I said. "He was never one of the mob."

"He was never married, either, and he's no kid."

"I—mentioned that to him last night, Sergeant. And he pointed out that I was single, too."

"You accused your client of being a homo? A hundred dollar a day client?"

"Not exactly. But when he first hired me, he insisted I investigate him as thoroughly as any suspect and I took him at his word."

Lehner frowned. "Puma, that sounds like you're almost honest. Wouldn't that be suicide in this business?"

"Sergeant," I said pompously, "complete honesty is suicide in any business, any marriage, any art or any relationship. I'm as honest as any in my profession and much more honest than the majority of them."

"You might be, at that. For some reason, I could never get to like you."

"I'm big and arrogant," I explained. "And free from a time clock. It's possible you envy me."

Silence. He finished his coffee and stood up. "Everything you know is in these daily reports you send in?"

I nodded.

"Keep sending them in."

I nodded. "Sergeant, I have no way of getting information from the Santa Monica Department. Would you pass on to me what you get from them?"

He nodded. Both of us had now lied to each other with nods, the mark of honest men.

He said, "Thanks for the coffee," and went out looking no happier than he had at his entrance.

They had a line on Jean Talsman now and that could lead to Mary. Under police questioning, she might admit she had never hired me. My current semi-cooperation from the Department would cease if they learned anything about that.

I studied my primitive art work with the tentative and obvious relationship lines. I crumpled it and threw it in the wastebasket. To all of them, an investigator was a resented alien and they showed him only the surface of their personalities. The truth was deeper; the truth of murder would be buried deepest of all.

Around twelve-thirty, I headed for Stormoff's, stopping at the bank on the way. I didn't think the twelve dollars I had in my wallet was enough insurance against the hazard of a hungry girl at Stormoff's.

The redhead was on time, arriving only a few minutes after I had. She wore a light green suit and her beautiful hair was piled high on her head. Not a masculine eye in the restaurant missed her. She ordered a double Martini and so did I. She relaxed in her chair and smiled at me as though we were friends.

"How's business?" I asked.

"It will go on. George was the genius, but the new boss is bright enough." She sipped some water. "By the way, one of our clients was asking about you this morning."

"Which one?"

"Dennis Greene. Do you know him?"

"I met him once. What did he want to know about me?"

"He never told me. He asked if I knew anything about you and I said I knew nothing and that ended that."

"Tell me, do you know much about him? I mean, is he—"

She smiled and nodded. "I'm certain he is. A waste, isn't it, such a rich and distinguished man without a woman to help spend his money."

"I asked," I explained, "because it was one of Greene's men who beat me up. And then, yesterday, we uncovered a homo angle in Tom Talsman's death."

"Tom Talsman?"

"Don't you know him?"

She shook her head. "Was that the man who was killed in Santa Monica yesterday?"

"That's right. He came to see you the night before last, but you weren't home."

Her eyes widened. I couldn't be sure if it was fright or amazement, but I was sure it wasn't deception.

I asked quietly, "Are you sure you don't know him?"

"I'm sure. Wait—isn't that the man you asked me about Sunday morning?"

"It could be. I've forgotten."

Silence. She sipped her drink and I sipped mine. Her face was more guarded now, her position in the chair more erect.

Finally, she asked, "How do you know this Talsman person came to see me when I wasn't home?"

"The police were following him," I lied. "I'm working closely with the Department on this business."

She finished her Martini and looked at me. I ordered two more. We talked about a number of things after that and according to her knowledge of the Ryerson client list, none of the doubtful citizens George had serviced were unduly dissatisfied with the relationship.

"There were chances," she said, "for George to engage in gouging and polite blackmail, but he resisted every one. I don't know if it was his honesty or the reputations of his clients that kept him on the side of the angels, though."

"You can't think of any client with whom he had an unsatisfactory relationship?"

She paused, thinking. "Well, perhaps Dennis Greene could be the exception. I don't know what it was, because George never talked about it, but there seemed to be an animosity between them."

"Why did Greene stay with him, then?"

"Because George was familiar with Greene's entire financial structure and that was important at tax time."

"You don't think it was Greene's—oddness that bothered Ryerson?"

"No. Dennis Greene wasn't our only unusual client. You must remember we have a lot of studio people." She sniffed. "I could get rich, writing for those exposé magazines."

"Maybe George did supply some of the magazines without your knowing it. Could that be possible?"

"It's possible, but I doubt it. At any rate, I haven't seen our clients mentioned in the magazines yet. And I doubt if the magazines would pay enough to George to make the possible loss of the client's account a sensible risk."

It was a good if expensive meal. Eileen Rafferty could be pleasant enough when she wanted to be and though I had learned very little for my money, it was good for my ego to sit in a fine restaurant with a girl as attractive as this one. The talk stayed trivial.

I drove her back to her office and she thanked me for the lunch and on impulse I asked her if it would be all right for me to phone her some evening.

"Why not?" she answered. "I haven't anything wealthier breaking down my door at the moment."

There was no reason for me to feel guilty as I drove back to the office. One weekend in Palm Springs didn't make me a married man, or even, as Mary had pointed out, an engaged one.

I had a right to line up future potentials.

TEN

THERE were nothing but ads in the afternoon mail and my phone answering service informed me there had been no calls while I was away.

I thought back on the lunch and one attitude of Eileen Rafferty's bothered me. She had not shown nearly enough interest in why Tom Talsman had come to see her; she had showed no concern about it after learning how I had come into possession of the information.

That could mean she had known why he had come to see her. If that were true, why had she been unfamiliar with his name when I had first mentioned it? It appeared reasonably certain that she was trying to hide her relationship with him.

Of course, I couldn't be positive that the death of Ryerson and the death of Talsman were connected. I was being paid only to investigate the death of Ryerson. Motive, motive, automotive . . .

Had Talsman been investigating the Ryerson murder? And for whom? And why had he hated Ross so? So far, the only connection between Ryerson and Tom Talsman was Jean. And yet, Talsman had tried to question Leslie Colt and had gone over to see Eileen Rafferty. That seemed to prove he was investigating Ryerson's murder. Why? If I could learn that, I would be closer to the final truth, but the man who could tell me why was dead.

I turned on my small radio for the three o'clock news report and learned that George Ryerson's estate had been estimated at close to four hundred thousand dollars. I wondered if that news would affect the marital attitude of Leslie Colt. George, it developed, had not only dabbled in figures. He had speculated in real estate and prospered in the current real estate boom.

From my bubbling subconscious, the phrase "remote from violence" came up to heckle me. Where had I read that? What did it mean to me now? Dennis Greene was remote from violence, insulated from the necessity of wounding by his thugs, remote from the wounding. That elegant man, dabbling in the rackets from an aloof wealth and protected from the throes of feminine fickleness by a mental quirk.

The phrase had come up from the same mental cavern that had produced the motive, motive, automotive teaser. A pattern my dull conscious mind couldn't find was being formulated in the subconscious. Jack Ross was remote from violence, too. Though Tom Talsman had tried to change that situation. And failed, as he so often did. Leonard the waiter? No.

In order to unlock a mystery, one needs a key. Tom Talsman had been one, I was now sure, and I had neglected to concentrate enough attention on him. The only apparent key left was Miss Eileen Rafferty and I decided she would not be neglected as Tom had been.

My phone rang and Mary said, "I thought you were going to call me."

"I was. It's only four o'clock."

"Okay. I want you for dinner. Jack and Jean will be here."

"I'm sorry. It's very important that I work tonight."

A silence, and then, "Puma, you're not annoyed with me?"

"Of course not."

"Or bored?"

"Never."

"Okay, then, you work. But be careful. Don't go flexing your muscles." A pause. "Does it look hopeful? Do you think you're getting somewhere?"

"Not at the moment. All I can do is plug along, snooping into this and that until something breaks."

"Something like your head. Or your ribs. I'm going to

talk to Jack Ross about you. I'll bet he could find you a much better job than the one you have."

"Don't. I've got the job I want."

A sigh. "All right, bull-head. Call me tonight if you get a chance to. I'm not sounding possessive, am I?"

"A little, but I don't mind. If it's at all possible, I'll phone you tonight."

I was lucky to have such a nice girl like me. Generally, women under sixty didn't and it made my love-life haphazard. The redhead had been nice to me, too, at lunch. Perhaps I was becoming more and more attractive as I grew older.

Dr. Dale Graves came in to say, "Little poker game tonight, Joe. Table stakes. Interested?"

"I have to work. And table stakes poker with professional men would be a little rich for my peasant blood."

"You're a professional man, too, in a sort of crummy way. Got an extra cigarette?"

"I always save one for you," I told him. "Dale, don't you ever get an urge to throw everything overboard and just take off for some tropical island and go native?"

He nodded and yawned. "Every evening about this time. How would you like to look into dirty mouths all day long?"

"So why don't we ever chuck it?"

He shrugged. "Habit. Or maybe we're gutless. Or maybe we're naive and we still believe in this civilization. What's got you down this afternoon?"

"Frustration. Padding about with questions and getting nowhere. Being sneered at by my financial betters."

"You're single. There's nothing to keep you from that tropical island. Why don't you take off?"

I didn't answer. I couldn't.

He smoked my cigarette and smiled at me. "That Eriksen I read about in the paper—you beat him up, didn't you?"

I didn't answer.

"Was he the one who was on your floor the other day?"

I shook my head. "That was Tom Talsman on the floor. He was murdered in Santa Monica yesterday."

"Wow! And you're bored?"

"Fed up, not bored. Disenchanted."

"It's the same thing. Puma, you need a weekend at Las Vegas. Or maybe a woman."

I stood up. "I think what I really need is a million dollars. Shall I give you another cigarette for later or are you going home now?"

He came over to pat my shoulder. "You maintain your sense of humor and it will save you. Carry on, buddy." At the doorway, he turned. "For what it's worth, I admire you and I envy you."

He had a point; I wouldn't want his job, though it maintained a fine home with a mammoth swimming pool and a wife who paid a hundred and fifty dollars for a cotton dress. And a semi-genius son who had his own pipe organ at the advanced age of nine. So nobody lives in heaven. Here. Yet.

I had an early dinner at Lachman's and another investigator I knew was at a booth alone so I shared it with him. His name was Don Kranski and he kidded me about all the publicity I was currently receiving.

I told him it hadn't brought any new business into the office and then asked him what he knew about Dennis Greene.

"Nothing beyond the obvious rumors," he said. "I know something about Ryerson, though. I put in a week on him for his widow."

"I wouldn't ask you to violate a confidence," I said, "so I'm quietly waiting."

"The receptionist," he went on. "That redhead. You and the Department sure as hell missed on her."

"How, please?"

"Her name. Don't you remember Big Bill Rafferty?"

"Sure. The former D.A., the one who blew his own brains out. Wasn't he involved in some big scandal?"

"That's right. His wife hired an investigator to check his marital fidelity and the investigator came up with enough for a grand jury. An honest man, Tim Hovde, like us, and so he took it all to the police. Remember Tim?"

"Only by legend. He's dead, isn't he?"

"Died two years ago. But to get back to my angle, this Ryerson and the redhead were like that, all right. And now consider this—Arno Eriksen was a muscle for Big Bill

Rafferty in a union extortion racket Big Bill ran as a sideline. Rafferty claimed he was only a legal advisor for the outfit, but the grand jury decided otherwise. And they had reason to."

"Don," I said, "thank you very much. The whole day looks brighter."

"You're welcome."

I asked, "Why would Mrs. Ryerson check her husband when she was engaged in a little extra-marital frolic herself?"

"Maybe she wasn't when I worked on that job. Though you know, if I was going to guess about her, I'd say she had quite a crush on Jack Ross. And I've heard a rumor that you're working for Ross."

"You heard right. Anything detrimental you know about him?"

Don smiled. "If I did, I wouldn't tell you. I remember what happened to Arno Eriksen."

"Once in my career," I said bitterly, "I lose my head and nobody will let me forget it."

"You poor boy," he said mockingly. "You poor, sad, undernourised little Italian boy. I'm bleeding for you."

When the check came, I picked it up. "Expenses," I assured him. "It's little enough for what you've given me tonight."

"It's little enough," he agreed, "but more than I expected."

Big Bill Rafferty . . . The man was as glamorous a legend in this town as Jimmy Walker was in New York. And almost as crooked. And Arno Eriksen had worked for him. Would Eileen Rafferty know her dad's former muscle man?

I went out to park on National Boulevard again, near the Santa Monica Airport. Her light was on and I saw movement behind the thin drapes, so I knew she was home, this time. I had been there about twenty minutes when an Imperial pulled to the curb in front of the triplex. I couldn't be positive from where I sat, but the man who got out of the car looked like Dennis Greene. There was nobody else in the car.

I sat and waited. If I had come here without meeting Don Kranski in the restaurant, I would have been worried about Eileen Rafferty getting a visit from Dennis Greene.

Now, I could assume she had been expecting him. They had a mutual friend, Arno Eriksen. That would be a heavy, not a tentative, line. I was almost positive it was Greene but made a note of the license number for later checking.

He hadn't been out of sight for two minutes before a green Buick Special came up the street to park behind the Imperial. A fairly short and extremely heavy man got out of the Buick and went up the walk that served the triplex.

From my vantage point, I couldn't be sure he was going to the Rafferty girl's apartment. He could have been one of the other tenants. But he had looked uncomfortably like Arno Eriksen. If it was Arno, he had been released from the hospital earlier than I had expected.

I sat and waited.

In about ten minutes, the man who looked like Eriksen came down the walk again. I waited for him to get into the Buick, but he didn't. He climbed into the Imperial.

This was getting complicated. Now, I guessed, Greene would come out and he and Eriksen would drive away in his car. I didn't guess it for long. The Imperial's lights went on and it started to swing in a U-turn as I ducked below the cowl to avoid their revealing glare. It moved past and turned left on the street behind me. I waited. Would Greene come out now and drive the Buick away? Had they decided to trade in the Rafferty apartment? This was a weird one.

And then, after a few more minutes, I began to see a pattern. Her's was the rear triplex and its rear door would be served by the alley, if there was an alley. There weren't many in this part of town, but I thought I remembered one from my last trip here. I was about to start the engine of my car when the redhead came down the walk. She went directly to the parked Buick and climbed in behind the wheel. I had to duck once more as her lights swung in another U-turn.

I began to perspire. I remembered how George Ryerson had been found in his car. I, too, made a U-turn. I came to the mouth of the alley in time to see the two cars. They were turning right at the far end as I entered this one. I came out at the far end in time to see them turning to the left, two blocks up the street. I didn't want to get too close, but it was important that I didn't lose sight of them. I took the chance and goosed the Plymouth.

I kept them in sight. National to Sepulveda and Sepulveda to Wilshire. Ahead was the grounds of the Veteran's Hospital and on Wilshire here, there was a big driving range. I was sure they hadn't come to hit golf balls. I wondered if they would turn toward the Veteran's Hospital. Both cars slowed and for a moment it seemed they were going to turn into the driving range parking lot. But they continued slowly on the right side of Wilshire. And then, half a block from the glare of the driving range floodlights, the Imperial pulled over to the curb and stopped. The Buick pulled ahead of it and waited, its engine still running.

It was fairly dark here and the traffic busy enough to keep the drivers intent on their own driving. The stocky man got out of the Imperial and went up to climb into the Buick. The Buick went gunning off into traffic.

I could have followed but there was no point to it, I was certain. I pulled to the curb behind the Imperial and went up to examine the car. Dennis Greene was lying on the floor in back and he wasn't making a sound. I reached down to feel for his pulse and he moaned. That was enough for me.

I ran for the driving range and a phone.

ELEVEN

LEHNER said, "Sapped a couple of times." He looked at the paper in his hand. "Rupture of the subcutaneous blood vessels and an extravasation of blood. Now what the hell does that mean?"

"Contusions," I said. "He's a young doctor. Is he sure it's nothing worse?"

"He's not sure of anything, yet. Except that Greene is conscious and won't talk. Why not?"

"Hoodlums never talk, do they? Not to the police."

"He hasn't been a hoodlum for a long time. Think I ought to phone Captain Jeswald?"

"That would have to be your decision, Sergeant." I looked around the small room. "All right to smoke in here?"

"If you want. I wish to hell that Rafferty woman would get here. I want you two face to face when I question her. You can stop any lie as she voices it."

"How about the license number of that Buick? Has that been identified yet?"

"No, damn it!" He got up from behind the small desk. "I'll go and goose 'em a little. You wait here. Throw your ashes on the floor."

I was lighting a cigarette when Eileen Rafferty came in, accompanied by a detective. She stared at me and at the detective.

I asked him, "Get Eriksen, too?"

He shook his head. "Where's Sergeant Lehner?"

"He'll be right back. He went to check something."

Eileen Rafferty asked me hoarsely, "Exactly what is all this about, Mr. Puma?"

"I've no idea, Ma'm," I answered. "The Sergeant will explain it to you, I'm sure, as soon as he gets back."

"You asked about somebody named Eriksen," she accused me. "Why did you ask that?"

I smiled. "A private matter, Red. A local joke."

She bit her lower lip and her eyes held a glint of tears.

The detective said, "The chair next to the desk, Miss Rafferty." He turned to me. "I suppose he'll want a stenographer?"

"I have no idea," I said.

Will he want a stenographer, should I call Jeswald . . . What did they think I was, a Department advisory board? I smoked my cigarette and stared at the floor.

Sergeant Lehner came in, glanced at Eileen Rafferty only briefly and sat down behind the desk. To the detective, he said, "Have Roberts sent in for dictation."

"He's not here, Sergeant. You could use the recorder."

"All right, all right. How about Eriksen?"

"Patton's still out on that."

"You get on it, too. I won't need you here."

The man left, and Lehner studied Eileen Rafferty.

"Well, Miss Rafferty, I imagine you have an interesting story to tell us."

"I have a request," she said. "I want to phone my lawyer."

"It might take some time for him to get here," he said easily. "Is there anything you don't feel free to talk about, Miss Rafferty?"

She didn't answer.

A man brought in a machine and set it on the desk. Lehner plugged it into the wall receptacle and connected a microphone. He didn't turn it on.

I asked, "How about my story, Sergeant?"

"Hers first," he said.

"I'm tired," I protested, as we had planned for me to protest. "I haven't been well since I left the hospital. I can't sit here all night. How about my coming back in the morning?"

"In that case," he said with a fine touch of ham, "we'd have to hold Miss Rafferty until you got back. And the newspapers would want to know why we were holding Big Bill Rafferty's daughter." He expelled his breath wearily. "I was hoping to avoid unnecessary publicity if possible."

Eileen Rafferty sat stiffly in her chair, glancing between us anxiously and suspiciously. Finally, she almost whispered, "Am I being threatened?"

Lehner shook his head absently. "Of course not. Well, there's the phone, Miss Rafferty. You can go, Puma. Tell the reporters they can come in now."

I stood up.

Eileen Rafferty said, "Just a second—wait, please—"

I sat down again. Lehner started the machine and set the microphone on its stand between him and Miss Rafferty.

"This evening," she said slowly, "Dennis Greene came to see me at my flat. I had never seen him anywhere but at the office and I was surprised at his visit. He asked me about Mr. Ryerson's death and if I knew why Mr. Puma was so interested in it. I didn't know anything about it and I said so. Only a few minutes after Mr. Greene came, someone else rang my bell and the man who was there told me he was Arno Eriksen and he used to know my father."

Lehner asked, "You didn't recognize him?"

She shook her head. "I was only seven years old when he had seen me last, he told me. He asked if Greene was there and said he wanted to talk with him." She paused. "Could I have a glass of water?"

Lehner frowned, muttered something, got up and left the room. Silence. Eileen Rafferty didn't look at me and I didn't look at her. I would have to scratch her as a boudoir potential. It seemed we were never going to be gay, laughing friends.

Lehner came back with a giant paper cup of water and handed it to her. She sipped it, said, "Thank you," and waited for him to be seated again.

Then she went on slowly. "I told Mr. Eriksen he could talk with Mr. Greene. Mr. Greene became highly agitated and finally suggested he and Mr. Eriksen talk in the backyard, as their business was certainly none of mine. They went out."

Lehner asked, "How do you mean—Greene became agitated?"

"Nervous, frightened."

"What did he say to make you think he was?"

"He didn't say anything like that. It was his—manner."

"Go on."

"They went out in the backyard. They were arguing loudly and I was afraid the neighbors would complain. I couldn't hear what they were talking about, though. Then there was a sudden silence."

She reached for the paper cup and sipped some more water. She was breathing heavily. "In a minute, Mr. Eriksen came back in and said Mr. Greene had had a heart attack and we had better get him out of the backyard at once."

"You didn't consider phoning for a doctor?"

She nodded quickly. "I did. But Mr. Eriksen told me that if Mr. Greene died, it would look very bad for me."

"Now why, Miss Rafferty?"

"Because Mr. Eriksen told me that Mr. Greene was the man who had—betrayed my father."

"Betrayed—?"

"I meant—informed on." She put a hand to her eyes. "He was the man who gave Mr. Hovde, that private investigator, the information that the grand jury acted on."

"Greene? Eriksen was lying to you, Miss Rafferty."

She took a deep breath. "I didn't know that. Then Mr. Eriksen said we could drive Mr. Greene over to the Veteran's Hospital as that was the closest. He promised to see I wouldn't be involved. He took Mr. Greene in the one car and I followed in Mr. Eriksen's."

"And—?"

"When Mr. Eriksen stopped on Wilshire, I thought he couldn't find the entrance to the hospital. I stopped in front of him and he came up to tell me Mr. Greene had recovered and was all right. I drove home and Mr. Eriksen left immediately."

Lehner sighed and looked at me. I shrugged.

Lehner said quietly, "That's some story, Miss Rafferty. But even with Norman Rockwell illustrations, I don't think there's a magazine in America that would buy anything like it."

She said nothing, staring at him stonily.

He said, "Certainly no police officer in America would buy it. Would you like to begin over with the truth?"

"It is the truth," she whispered.

Lehner looked at me questioningly.

I said, "Sergeant, if you'll get me a glass of fresh water, I'll do my damnedest to dream up a better story."

Eileen Rafferty said, "I want to phone my lawyer."

"You certainly need one," Lehner agreed. He pushed the phone toward her. "Ask for an outside line." He leaned back in his chair. "On the surface, Puma, her story matches yours."

"On the surface," I answered, "a street over a sewer looks exactly like one that isn't over a sewer. She must have figured how much I had seen from outside and tailored her story to that."

Lehner nodded thoughtfully.

"But," I said, as we had rehearsed it, "we've still got Greene, haven't we? And a few things Miss Rafferty doesn't know I know."

He nodded in mock satisfaction. "Haven't we, though? Well, it's enough for a case. Can't you get your number, Miss Rafferty?"

Miss Eileen Rafferty gave no indication of being impressed by our theatrical abilities. She went steadily about her task of phoning her attorney.

Behind my eyes, the headache grew. I said, "I don't suppose we'll get any place until Greene is ready to dictate that story he told you. I'd like to go home, Sergeant."

"All right. Don't you want protection? Eriksen is still out there, prowling around, remember."

I shook my head wearily. "I'll drop in bright and early tomorrow, Sergeant."

I stood up and went to the door to deliver my exit line. "What bothers me, Sergeant, is how Eriksen, fresh from the hospital, had the strength to get Greene into that car all by himself."

"It bothers me, too," he admitted. "I'm surprised it doesn't bother Miss Rafferty. You'd think she'd want to help an old friend of her father's." A fine ironic note to make my exit on.

In the hallway, Detective Deering asked, "Any luck in there, Joe?"

"Not yet."

Deering smiled. "She's a cool one. I was with Patton when he picked her up. That dame's a pro, Joe."

"So was her father and he didn't make it."

"Sure, but he didn't have her build. Take it easy, sonny boy."

I promised him I would and went out to the Plymouth. Silly as her story was, we couldn't prove it wasn't true right now. Maybe we would never be able to.

And if Greene didn't cooperate, what could the Department hold her on? This was a murder case under investigation, not a backyard quarrel. She could swear she had never seen the bludgeoned Greene in the rear of that Imperial and who could prove she had? The proximity of the Veteran's Hospital to the driving range was just a coincidence but she had used it to add credence to her story. She was not a stupid woman, this Eileen Rafferty.

She had been Ryerson's girl friend and undoubtedly in his confidence. All the files containing the financial shenanigans of the shady Ryerson clients had been open to her scrutiny. Big Bill Rafferty's daughter would know how to milk a nickel from that, if she was a true daughter.

Eriksen was still out in the darkness somewhere, prowling around, but it didn't keep me from falling asleep immediately. I didn't open my eyes until nine o'clock in the morning.

I wanted something better than packaged cereal and frozen orange juice this morning; I ate breakfast in Beverly Hills.

There was a picture of Eileen Rafferty in the *Times,* and the account of last night's disturbance identified her as the daughter of a former district attorney. The *Times* did not call him "Big Bill" anywhere in the article. Arno Eriksen had not been apprehended when this paper had been printed. I could guess that he was still at large.

I phoned the Hollywood Station from my office and asked for Captain Jeswald. When I got him, I asked if Greene was still under medical observation.

"No. He went home early this morning. Sergeant Lehner is here; he can tell you anything you want to know, Joe."

Lehner told me what I'd expected to hear; Greene would file no complaint. I said, "You have his unlisted phone number, undoubtedly."

"I have. What's on your mind?"

"Maybe he'd feel less—restricted if he talked with me. After all, I'm the man who phoned the doctor for him."

"And you then put everything that happened into your report to us?"

"Not everything, Sergeant. Everything that applies to the case we're working on. Greene may tell me something he doesn't want repeated. If I don't stay private, remember, I don't stay solvent. Give me some latitude."

A momentary silence and then his friendly voice. "All right. I guess you've given me enough reason to trust you, Joe." He gave me the number, and I hung up, warmed. It was the first time Sergeant Lehner had ever called me by my first name.

My mail consisted of an ad from a local brokerage house and an expense check from Mrs. Dora Diggert. The check was small but so had my expenses been. It was check number nine on the Westwood Branch of the Bank of America, my own favorite.

It was almost eleven and Dennis Greene should be up. I phoned the unlisted number and a pleasant, rather high male voice informed me this was the Dennis Greene residence.

"This is Joseph Puma," I said. "I'd like to speak with Mr. Greene."

"He's resting, sir. If you care to leave your number, I will be sure to inform Mr. Greene you called when he wakens."

I left my number and went to work on finishing up my report for yesterday. He phoned back as I was finishing. He told me he would be in my neighborhood this afternoon, and if I wanted to see him, he could drop in. I told him I would be in the office. He thanked me for my part in his rescue last night and said he would be in around two o'clock.

My still-warm phone rang again and this time it was my Mary.

"What about that redhead in this morning's paper, Puma? How did you get tangled up with her?"

"Involved," I said gently, "not tangled. You are being vulgar. She is an evil girl and I will have nothing to do with evil girls and you know it. How's Jean bearing up?"

"Better. Seriously, Joe, what was all that about?"

"I can't tell you any more than you read in the paper. I'm not working for you, kid. I'm working for Jack."

"He'll tell me. He'll tell me anything. He's a born gentleman."

"He can afford to be. What did you do last night?"

"Moped, mostly. Why don't you come here for lunch? Or we could meet somewhere in Beverly Hills?"

"What about the funeral?"

"There isn't going to be any. Only the cremation. I asked a Catholic friend and it's a sin, Joe. I should have talked Jean out of it."

"It's not your business," I said. "About the lunch, I'd like it, but I'd be bad company. And somebody very important is going to be here around two o'clock. I don't want to miss him so I think I'll grab a sandwich at the drug store."

Silence and then, "Joe, you are bored with me."

"Never," I told her earnestly. "If the man I'm meeting is at all cooperative, it's possible I'll have a lead that can clean this whole mess up. Then we'll be ready for our weekend at Jack's."

"The good life, eh? I'm glad to see you're learning to compromise."

"I've been for rent for so long," I told her, "I decided I might as well be for sale. You stay out of trouble, now."

"Natch," she said. "I'm saving myself for you." She laughed, and hung up.

I didn't feel nearly as sorry for myself this morning as I had yesterday. Mary loved me and Lehner had called me Joe and I had a rich friend in Palm Springs.

Talsman was now, or soon would be, ashes. George Ryerson was surrounded by the cold, damp ground. I was alive and functioning. If that continued until being alive and functioning was no longer important, I would not ask for the immortality Mary was so concerned about. I would figure I had been given a full share of what was available.

I sat alone in my inexpensive office wondering if I actually believed what I was trying to. And I wondered if a man ever reached an age where it wasn't important to be alive. A sane man. The sound of Dr. Graves' busy drill came to me and reminded me this world was not heaven. If there was a heaven, this was not it. A thought I had had yesterday. When a pretty woman no longer interested me, I decided finally, I would then be ready for Forest Lawn.

At twelve-thirty, I had a sandwich at the drug store and picked up a paperback western from the rack to take back to the office. I never outgrew my love for westerns. I was hunkering over a small fire in the middle of the immeasurable plain under the clear stars with my wide-shouldered hero when Dennis Greene entered my office. He was alone. A square patch of surgical gauze was taped to his head above his ear and one eye was almost closed, surrounded by blue-black, swollen flesh.

"Nice boy, that Eriksen," I said. "Isn't he the man you retained the sentimental interest in?"

Dennis Greene didn't smile. He sat in my customer's chair and looked at me gravely. "You work with the police, Mr. Puma?"

"Mostly. I carefully explained to one of them this morning, though, that I couldn't and wouldn't repeat everything you told me. Unless it's connected with the Ryerson murder."

"That's why I'm here," he said. "Though I personally had nothing to do with the Ryerson murder." He leaned back and lighted a cigarette. "I lied to you about Arno Eriksen. I don't have any interest in his welfare, except to hope he has a heart attack. He has been black-mailing me intermittently and successfully for seven years. I was interested in him only in the hope I could learn from you that he was involved in the Ryerson murder. That way, I'd have something to trade for his silence other than money."

"I see. Yesterday morning, when you dropped into Ryerson's office, did you inquire about me from Eileen Rafferty?"

He stared at me. "I swear to you I didn't. Nor was I anywhere near that office yesterday. Why should she tell you that?"

"Who knows? Maybe, to lead me off her trail. And you did the same thing by showing this sentimental interest in Eriksen. Why did you go to see Miss Rafferty late last night?"

"Frankly, to frighten her. I knew she was involved romantically with George Ryerson and that Eriksen used to work for her father. To me, she looked like a girl who could know something about Ryerson's death, and if that knowledge involved Arno Eriksen, I wanted it, and if I couldn't frighten it out of her, I would buy it."

"Then Eriksen actually never worked for you?"

"I didn't say that and I won't answer it either way. I'm here to tell you I might have more contacts who could locate Arno than you have. I couldn't personally turn him over to the police, you understand. You could."

"And if I did? What would they hold him on? You refused to sign a complaint."

"He could be questioned about the Ryerson murder. Why else would he be working with Eileen Rafferty?"

"Mr. Greene," I said patiently, "you're not making sense and you know it. Miss Rafferty has already been questioned about the Ryerson murder—and released. What you wanted was for me to go after Arno Eriksen and not bring him in to the police, wasn't it?"

He lifted his chin. "Maybe. You worked him over once, didn't you? Another time wouldn't hurt."

"It would hurt me. And he isn't the kind you can beat

the truth out of. Last time, after that beating, he lied. He said he was working for Tom Talsman, when actually he was working for Miss Rafferty."

"Are you sure of that?"

"Not completely."

"They could have all been working with one another, you know."

I nodded and took a breath. "You wouldn't know if Eriksen is homosexual or not, would you?"

There was only the slightest of pauses before he answered mildly, "I wouldn't know. Why?"

"Because there's reason to believe the person who killed Tom Talsman was. Another question, did you and Eriksen go into the backyard to argue last night?"

"Yes."

"Then, perhaps Miss Rafferty honestly didn't know you had been slugged. And possibly Eriksen only came there because he was following you."

"Arno didn't come there only because he was following me. As soon as he walked in, he asked her, in surprise, what I was doing there."

"She seemed to know him?"

"She let him in without asking his name or his business, as though they were old friends."

"And what did you quarrel about in the yard?"

"He wanted to know what I was doing there. I told him I was interested in the death of George Ryerson. He swung at me and I tried to protect myself and the lights went out."

"And you think you know where he is now?"

"I think I can find out."

I said, "Last night, Eileen Rafferty told the police that you were the man who had informed on Big Bill Rafferty. She said Arno Eriksen had told her that."

"It's a lie," Dennis Greene said evenly, "and I don't believe Eriksen told her that. Why would he?"

I didn't answer.

After a silence of a few seconds, Greene said earnestly, "If you can prove Arno Eriksen guilty of murder, I'll pay you five thousand dollars."

"You don't mean I should frame him, do you, Mr. Greene?"

"You've heard my offer. If he is convicted of murder

through any efforts of yours, fair or foul, I'll pay you five thousand dollars. I'll pay it in cash, tax-free money, sir. That's a lot of money, tax-free."

"To a poor man, it's a fortune," I said. "And I'm a poor man. For that kind of money, in the old days, you could get a dozen men killed."

"These aren't the old days," he said. He stood up.

I looked at him musingly. "You're very bitter, Mr. Greene."

"I've been humiliated. If I get any word of Arno's whereabouts, I'll let you know immediately. What happens from there on would be in the laps of the gods."

"You could hope he'd pull a gun on me, eh? And I'd have to kill him?"

His smile was brief. He said good-by and went out. I watched him go, wondering if Eileen Rafferty had helped drag him to the car last night. I don't know why I should have thought of that.

But I was mighty glad I did. Because it sent the first hopeful gleam of light into the darkness of my dull brain. Motive, motive, automotive . . .

It was beginning to make sense.

TWELVE

THE CASTERS on that heavy mop pail had tried to tell me, but I had overlooked the obvious. That pail would be too heavy to handle without casters.

Unfortunately, murders may be guessed at in the field but they are proven in courts of law. Could I go to the murderer now and say, "Everything points to you; you might as well confess"?

I could. If this was a movie or television play. Because there, the murderer would answer, "You got me, and seeing how you got me, I might as well confess in great detail to you how everything happened as it will help the D.A."

Life should be more like the movies. Or TV. Or anyway,

like an English-type deductive mystery. Things would be simpler. But in this cynical age, if you found the murderer with the gun in his hand and the corpse at his feet, he would say, "Okay, wise guy, prove it! I got me an expensive lawyer and you got an overworked D.A. Try and prove it!"

Before most of the juries you find today, you would be lucky to prove you were alive, unless your lawyer was expensive. I would need to break down someone close to the killer, someone who could be prompted to betray the killer for money or out of self-interest. I didn't know how much money Ross would pay. Motive, means and opportunity. Motive, who would know it? Means and opportunity, who could prove either?

I phoned Captain Horace Jeswald and asked him, "Anything new out of Santa Monica? You promised to keep me informed."

"Only some fingerprints. We had nothing to match them here so we sent them to Washington. Is that useful information?"

"It might be the most important of all if I brought in a killer."

"Are you planning to?"

"Eventually, I suppose. You released the Rafferty girl, didn't you?"

"You can blame Greene for that. Did you talk with him?"

"I did. He offered me five thousand dollars if I could prove Eriksen was a murderer. He claimed that he, Greene I mean, had nothing to do with Ryerson's murder."

"I see. How do you plan to frame Eriksen?"

"Captain," I said sadly. "Brother. A certain wealthy man I know is going to try to locate Eriksen for me."

"Greene?"

"I didn't say it. His vanity must be great, don't you think? I wouldn't go to five grand for revenge on a man who merely blackened one of my eyes."

"You haven't got five grand. And probably never will have. Well, if you get Eriksen, you know where to bring him."

"Hell, yes. To the Venice Station. That's where he lives."

"Don't live so dangerously, Joe. I'll see that the news

photographer gets your good side. They don't know your profile at the Venice Station like I do."

He must have had a good night; he rarely indulged in humor, even humor as sad as the above. He was a good man. Pompous and self important, dull and tedious, but well fitted for his job.

Motive, motive, automotive, means and opportunity. There was still a rough road ahead. I was playing with moneyed people who could afford expensive lawyers, lawyers who could prove black was white.

Big Bill Rafferty must have left a sizable estate if he was as clever as his legend pictured him. And though his daughter worked for a living, it was possible she had worked for Ryerson after she had become the woman in his life. Perhaps she only worked to be near him. Or more probably, she worked where there were outside dollars to be made. She could be the kind of sensible girl who didn't believe in living on her principal.

If I hurried, I would still have time to get to the bank before it closed.

From the bank, it was only a few blocks to Mary's apartment, so I drove over there. She and Ross were in the living room; Jean was taking a nap in the bedroom.

"Stranger," Mary said. "What brings you in?"

"The need for information." I looked at Ross. "Could I speak with you alone for a few seconds?"

He yawned and stretched. "Important? What about, Joe?"

"Important," I said.

He stood up and said to Mary, "If he makes any advances, I'll holler."

We went out to the hall.

When we came back in again, Mary was studying me curiously.

I said to her, "Will you come out in the hall now?"

She looked at Jack and he shrugged. She stood up and came out to the hall with me.

There, I said, "I don't want you to blow up, now. I'm going to ask you a very personal question."

"I'll try to stay calm. Is it the same question you asked Jack?"

"No. It's about Jean and that's why I don't want Jack to hear it. Now think carefully before you answer the question."

She nodded, waiting.

"Did Jean Talsman, at any time, display any homosexual tendency around you?"

The brown eyes flared and she started to speak.

"Wait," I said quickly. "She's not a suspect in this case. I want you to think particularly of any time when she came home drunk. Perfectly normal, or apparently normal, people occasionally have lapses of that kind under alcohol."

Again, Mary started to speak. And stopped. Then, softly, "This is very important, isn't it, Joe?"

"Of course. Or I wouldn't ask such a question."

"There was one time," she whispered, "when she came home drunk and acted—strange. That—way, you know? She insisted on sleeping with me and, well—I assumed she was so drunk she thought I was a man. She fell asleep after I pushed her away."

"Thank you," I said. "It's only another straw in the wind, but it helps to build my theory."

Mary put a hand on my shoulder. "You'll never mention this to Jack, will you?"

"Of course not." I kissed her forehead. "I'll see you. Think of me, when you're not busy."

She nodded absently. "Joe, people can't be just partly that way, can they?"

"Yes. Some are, and some are all the way. Some can't help it and some can. Some arrive at it early and some late and for a variety of complex reasons. Now, don't brood about it. It's not a pleasant topic. Think of normal, lustful people like you and me."

"Joe, don't rush off. Jack Ross never married. What's the reason?"

"Relax," I said. "Don't try to pump me. I'll phone you tomorrow morning, probably."

"I'm nervous," she said. "I'm going to be more so."

I kissed her again, patted her cheek and left her. Her door didn't close until I got to the bottom of the staircase.

Straws, as I had told her, but all blowing the same direction. To the Tulare kid, this sort of revelation would be more sickening than to the sophisticated city-bred. Not that the ratio of these half-people was any lower in the small towns, just the number of them. I was a big town boy, myself. Fresno.

And for a variety of reasons . . . That had been told to me by a psychologist friend and it led me to *motive,* the first of the necessary and deadly triplicate.

There was a possibility that after last night's disturbance, Eileen Rafferty had not gone to work this morning. If so, she could be home now. It was not quite four o'clock.

She was home. She came to the door, looked at me bitterly, and started to close the door.

"Two have died," I warned her. "You could be next on the list."

"You don't fool me or frighten me," she said scornfully. "You don't know anything and you're trying to get by on bluff and bluster."

"Please listen to me, Miss Rafferty. You're not as safe as you think you are. You underestimate the law. The Department is big and complex and overworked. But the boys keep grinding away and eventually they get to the truth. It's only a question of time."

"So is living," she said, and closed the door.

The first time I had come here, she had asked if I was armed. She hadn't asked this time; I no longer frightened her. She knew I wasn't working for the killer.

I went back to the office and my phone answering service informed me there had been a message from a Mr. Battered. That was Dennis Greene's kind of humor.

Mr. Eriksen, the monotone of the operator revealed, could be found at the Vicente Motel under the pseudonym of Ned Stevens. She gave me the address of the motel and told me there had been no other calls. I had passed the Vicente Motel going from the Bluffview bank to Mary's apartment. I seemed to be going in circles. I hoped, before the day was finished, I would complete the big circle I had started.

The manager of the motel told me there was a Ned Stevens in unit fourteen but he didn't know if Mr. Stevens was in now. I went down to ring the bell of unit fourteen and there was no answer. I parked in front and waited. Arno would probably no longer be driving the Buick, unless he had changed the plates. But it wouldn't be dark for a while yet and I might see him drive in.

If he had Dennis Greene on the hook, he could have a fairly steady source of income. He was getting too old to play his former game; there were younger, tougher boys eager to take his place. When Eileen Rafferty had summoned him from retirement, she must have convinced him there would be big money in the operation.

Traffic grew heavier as the sun moved further toward the western horizon. Three cars drove into the motel courtyard in that time but all of them were couples.

It was just starting to get dark and the manager had lighted his red neon Vacancy sign when a Plymouth of the same vintage as mine drove off the street into the yard.

My quarry had come home. I waited until the door of number fourteen closed behind him.

When I rang, he called out "Who's there?" and I answered "Joe Puma."

He opened the door and looked at me blankly. "I'm not armed. It didn't seem bright to be armed for a while. If you came to fight, beat it."

"I just want to talk, Arno. We're even, aren't we? You put me in the hospital and I returned the favor. Doesn't that make us even?"

"I play to win, not to get even. What do you have on your mind?"

"The death of George Ryerson."

"I don't know anything about it."

"Your friend does. She's an amateur, Arno. She tries to act like a pro but she's never been tested."

He looked at me skeptically. "You rodded up?"

"The case seemed to need it. I didn't plan to use it here, though. How can a little talk hurt you, Arno? It might save you some lumps later."

"Come in," he said.

The room held a bed and three chairs. I sat on a chair near the door. He went over to sit on the bed.

I said, "Miss Rafferty knows who killed Ryerson. I would bet on that."

"Well, I don't. And I'm not interested. And let me tell you something more, peeper, I'm all for her. Her old man was the greatest guy I ever knew. He took care of his boys. He knew what these punks today can't learn—he knew what loyalty meant."

"Okay. But he's dead. Did you know that Eileen Rafferty and George Ryerson were lovers? George's wife knows that. She hired a detective to find it out for her."

"Who was the peeper, you?"

"No, a friend of mine. I have a lot of friends and quite a few of them are in the Police Department, Arno. Why don't you get out of this extortion racket now? That way you'll get out whole and well."

He sneered. "Come off it. You think working for Dennis Greene will keep you on the right side of the law? You're crazy."

"I don't work for Greene. I work for Jack Ross and if you think I'm lying, check me. I'll give you a number right now where he can be reached."

"To hell with Jack Ross," he said. "You pulled that gag before."

"All right. Then consider I'm working with the Los Angeles Police Department on this. Because Greene wouldn't sign a complaint, the Department isn't too interested in you right now. But they would pick you up as a matter of routine. Why not come clean with me and avoid all that bother?"

"I know my loyalty, Puma. Don't talk cop to me; it's a dirty word. And I'll tell you something else—you're whistling in the dark. You don't know who did what to who, or why. You're all mouth and muscle."

"Okay, Arno. And you're a brain?"

"I never had to be. But I can spot a brain when I come across one, and you don't fill the bill."

"I gave you your chance," I warned him. "You're being stupid."

"Drop dead," he said contemptuously.

"You're fighting the money," I said patiently. "Big Bill didn't teach you much. The first thing a hoodlum should learn is never to fight the money. Money's always right, Shortie."

"Maybe Red and I know where it is. Mouth isn't money. How would a cheap working stiff like you know anything about money?"

"It is only the wealthy people who can afford private investigators," I explained to him. "Or the big firms. All of the clients I ever had were wealthy."

I stood up. "Don't you want your out?"

He looked at me suspiciously. "My out? Who are you to offer me an out?"

I sighed. "I figured you were getting old enough to retire. I figured you would have the sense to jump at a chance to get out of this mess clean."

He laughed, and called me a name.

I took out my gun and said wearily, "You had your chance. Now, don't make a move. I'm working with the Department and I'd be completely in the clear if you should get shot resisting arrest."

I picked up his phone and called the Hollywood Police Station.

THIRTEEN

I SHOULD have been home an hour ago," Captain Jeswald said pevishly. "I thought I'd wait around to see if Eriksen has anything new to tell us. I guess he never will."

"He's loyal to the Rafferty girl, because of her father," I explained. "I guess this Big Bill Rafferty had some mighty loyal co-workers, didn't he?"

"Big Bill didn't kill Ryerson. And this is a Police Department, not a historical research unit, Puma. What have you got? Nothing."

"Yet. Could you hold Eriksen overnight?"

"Why?"

"To keep him out of my hair. I like to keep as many pros off the opposing team as I can. I haven't the resources to fight professionals. I'm not big, like the Department." I rubbed my neck. "So I have to work longer hours and find what few allies I can."

"I bleed for you. Quit crying on my shoulder. We'll hold the bastard overnight."

"Thanks," I said. "And where's your phone book? Or city directory. I just thought of something."

"Who do you want to look up now?"

"A husband," I said. "She must have been married once."

He was a tall, thin man, a realtor and he had a small office on Ventura. It was only a shack, but he seemed to have a sizable list. His Cadillac, in the empty lot next to the office, was this year's model.

"Three kids," he told me, "and a wonderful wife, and here I am, still in the office at eight o'clock. Why?"

"So you can get rich and retire before you're fifty. How long were you married to your first wife?"

"Six months. I could have had it annulled and she wouldn't be able to use my name. But I tried to be a gentleman about it."

"That's our trouble," I admitted, "we try to be gentlemen. It costs us too much. Why do you think a woman like that would marry you in the first place?"

"Why do any of 'em marry? To make 'em look normal and respectable. I guess we all want to conform, right? Do you want me to call off a list of married queers who live right here in the Valley?"

"Nope. You're sure about your first wife, are you?"

He looked at his desk. "I'm sure. I caught her at it. Man, what a body, what a waste!" His eyes were reminiscent.

I thanked him and left him with his dreams and his new Cadillac. I could have used the phone in his office but it would have seemed in bad taste, somehow. I phoned from a filling station.

She said, "What now? I don't need you around any more."

"I have something very important to tell you and I don't know your address. It isn't anything I'd want to say over the phone."

A momentary pause and she gave me the address I'd asked for.

It was a low, sprawling house with a shake roof and antiqued barn siding. It was built on a knoll overlooking the Brentwood Country Club, about twenty-five hundred feet of house. I would estimate it as worth from fifty to a hundred thousand dollars. Out here, it's difficult to appraise real estate these days.

It was close enough to the Bluffview Branch of the Security-First National Bank to make that the logical choice of any resident interested in banking convenience.

She opened the door to me and said, "I hope you're not bringing trouble, Puma. I've had my fill of that lately."

I didn't answer.

She led me to a living room which combined contemporary with traditional in a style that indicated she had hired a decorator and the decorator had gone strictly by the book.

I sat on a satin-covered davenport and she sat on the same piece of furniture about three feet away. "Drink?" she asked.

"No, thanks, Mrs. Diggert. When you changed your account from the Bluffview bank to the Westwood one, you should have continued with the old numbering systems on your checks. The low number on the check you sent me suggested it must be a new account."

"Is there something wrong with the check? Didn't it clear?"

"I came about something else, about the death of George Ryerson. I suppose, if I had known where you lived, the proximity of this house to the Bluffview shopping center would have started me off on the right trail."

"You're not making any kind of sense, Puma."

"Wait," I said wearily, "and I'll try to. All I had was your unlisted number and your two hundred dollars. Your concern for Jean Talsman seemed like a normal attitude, then."

I thought I could hear her breathe. I looked up to see that her face was rigid, her eyes apprehensive.

I said, "When you assured me Jean was a very close, personal friend of yours, I took the expression at its face value. When you told me that Eileen Rafferty had phoned you, you hadn't yet learned how close she was to George Ryerson, had you?"

Her voice was tight. "You're talking gibberish. I'm not following you at all."

I ploughed on. "You didn't realize that Miss Rafferty was more than an employee to Ryerson and that he would tell her he was coming to see you when he broke the luncheon engagement. He was coming here to get this mess straightened out about Jean. He didn't want any trouble with the police and that's what your interference threatened to bring him. He came here."

She whispered, "He did not!"

"And when he explained to you that the man Jean had gone to was Jack Ross, you went over the edge, emotionally. You had enough reason to hate Jack Ross; he had learned you were—sick, and that's why he hadn't married you. You hated George for what he'd done, but you couldn't kill him here. He'd be too heavy for you to move all alone and you certainly didn't want him found here. You suggested he drive you to the bank. For what reason? Did you suggest paying him for something?"

"You're insane," she said, "completely insane. Are you trying to blackmail me?"

I asked quietly, "Why not? When you got to the parking lot and saw it was deserted, you had your perfect chance. You shot him with a gun that makes very little noise." I looked at her questioningly. "Were you drunk? You're drunk right now, aren't you?"

She said nothing, glaring at me.

I said, "You wanted Jean to stop dating and be a partner, didn't you? But not until you had degraded her to a point where she would be a physical partner, too. That's one of the roads to what you were trying to make her, isn't it—degradation? There are others, but that's one you used, isn't it?"

"You're filthy," she said. "You're rotten."

"You should have had your first marriage annulled, Mrs. Diggert. Then I wouldn't have known about Mr. Diggert. I talked with him an hour ago."

She seemed to shrink on the davenport next to me. She began to cry. "Are you trying to destroy me?"

"No. When Talsman came here, looking for his sister, you convinced him there was something evil about Jack Ross. You probably told Tom Talsman you had big executive plans for Jean. Did you tell the Rafferty girl that, too? Is she moving in, or will she be a silent partner?"

"You don't know anything. You can't prove anything. You're guessing at all of this, aren't you?"

"Mostly. Tom worked for you, trying to get his sister back. But when he learned why you wanted her back, it sickened him, and he must have finally realized you were the one who killed Ryerson. That's why he shouted that accusation at you in his apartment."

"You don't know anything, you don't know anything—" She was leaning forward, swaying, repeating the words over and over in a whisper.

"You killed Tom. Miss Rafferty pointed out to you how silly it was to use amateurs when you could get a professional thug. She brought Eriksen into it. Eriksen wouldn't have to know about Ryerson; Miss Rafferty had his complete loyalty."

Dora Diggert took a deep breath and looked at me stonily. "If you were sure about any of these things, you would have brought a police officer along."

"I might have. You stayed remote from violence, didn't you, using Talsman and Eriksen and the Rafferty girl? Well, money will buy almost anything. If there's enough money."

"There's enough money," she said quietly, "but you haven't anything to sell."

"Maybe not," I agreed. "Well, somebody might be interested in a theory." I stood up.

"Wait. You can't prove murder, but the other— I could pay a little something for your silence about—the other. I thought you always worked with the police?"

"I'm usually forced to. Mrs. Diggert, the police have a fingerprint from Tom Talsman's apartment, the fingerprint of a killer. All they need is a suspect to match it to. Are you willing to make that test?"

She stared at me. "You're lying."

"Why don't we run down to the Hollywood Station and try it on for size? Come on, I'll drive."

A long and heavy silence.

Then Dora Diggert said, "I deal in cash. George Ryerson, with his bookkeeper's mind, didn't realize the advantage of that. We quarreled about it quite often. He liked to threaten me with exposure from time to time. But that would be bad advertising, despite his informer's fee from the Internal Revenue Department. Would you like to see what ten thousand dollars looks like in real cash, Mr. Puma?"

"It would be interesting," I said. "Why don't you bring all your money out, and we can count it?"

She smiled for the first time, a weak and still doubtful smile. She said, "That would be fun. Tell me, as a professional, what do you think of Eileen Rafferty?"

"She's still an amateur. The first time I visited her at home, she asked me if I was armed. Why would I be, just visiting her? Unless I was still working for you, as I had been, and I had come to muscle her. If I wasn't working for you, which I wasn't by that time, her remark would let me know she had reason to fear you. That's a lead to you and the kind of tip-off pros avoid. It's better to make no casual remark."

"That's—rather involved."

"It's only a straw. This is a case composed almost entirely of straws. But once the police have enough straws to show the direction of the wind, they will have the fingerprint to prove your presence in Tom Talsman's apartment."

"You put together all these straws. Why is it they haven't, too, by this time?"

"There are too many murders," I told her, "and not enough policemen."

"You're bright," she said after a second. "You're much brighter than I first imagined you were. I could use a bright man on a retainer, Mr. Puma." She stood up, once again the poised and thinking business-woman. In command, once more.

She said lightly, "I'll go and get some money to show you."

Had I offered to sell out? I had schmaltzed around, talking money, but I hadn't actually said I would sell out.

She came back in, two minutes later, carrying a small grip. If that was full of bills of a respectable denomination, it could contain what a poor man would consider a fortune.

She opened the grip on the davenport and began to take out packets of currency. They were only ten dollar bills, but they were in packets and there were a lot of packets.

I wondered if she had a different grip for each denomination, like the Iowa farmers.

When she had piled a sizable share of the bills neatly on the satin, she said softly, "That's ten thousand dollars in tens. Of non-taxable income. Wonderful, isn't it, Mr. Puma?"

"Beautiful color," I said, "and fine engraving. But I guess it's time to stop playing games, Mrs. Diggert. Ten thousand isn't my price."

She asked thoughtfully, "What is, Mr. Puma?"

"I guess I'll never know," I answered. "I suppose if someone offered ridiculous figures, high in the millions, even the saints would sell out. But I'm sure no individual I know has enough money to make me betray my profession. I guess the time has come to go down and talk with the police, don't you think?"

"No," she said, "I don't." Her hand made one more trip to the grip and came out holding a small but deadly automatic.

"My God," I said, "you're an amateur, too. If that's the .25 calibre gun that killed Ryerson, you should have buried it."

"It's the only one I have," she told me, "and I thought I might need it. I was right, wasn't I?"

I saw her finger tightening and I knew it was too late to go for my own gun. I scrambled up and tried to leap over the back of the davenport.

I felt a sting and heard a *splat*. The sting was on that section of my anatomy which had only recently reposed on satin, a very undignified place to be hit.

Behind the davenport, I got my own .38 out and crawled quickly to the other end. Another *splat* sent stuffing flying from the davenport as I crawled clear of the back and stood up.

I couldn't shoot her. There is some inherent gentility in me that prevents me from shooting at a woman. I threw the .38 at her head as she turned my way.

Luckily, my aim was good.

Lehner said, "I'm supposed to be at the fights. If I'd been called two minutes later, I would have been gone."

"It's a lousy fight," I consoled him. "And this could get

you some ink. I'll be sure to mention you often to the reporters."

He sat down behind the desk in the room and looked at the reports that had been brought in. "The prints match. I guess, the way it looks now, this Rafferty dame is going to break down before Mrs. Diggert. I figured the Rafferty girl for the toughest one between those two, didn't you?"

"No," I said. "Sergeant, you know the best amateur in the world is nothing measured against even a prelim pro. Mrs. Diggert is a pro."

"Sit down," he told me. "You'll be here for quite a while yet."

"I can't sit down. It will be a few days before I'll be able to achieve that. Superficial, that wise doc called it. I wish he had it."

Lehner looked at me with a compassion alien to his hard face. "If you're really feeling bad, you could come back tomorrow, Joe."

"I'm feeling embarassed but not bad. How about Eriksen? When do you think he'll get smart enough to open up and save his own neck?"

"He'll never open up. But when the Rafferty girl cracks, he'll be implicated enough to get him a year or two, maybe. It depends on the jury. We don't worry about him; it's this Diggert we want to nail and this print is solid enough to give us reason for working on her in relays."

A detective came in and said, "That Rafferty girl is about ready to break, Sergeant. Want to come in and get the story with us?"

Lehner nodded and looked at me. "Want to come, Joe? You're the man who broke it; you ought to be in at the curtain."

"Not me," I said. "I don't like to listen to confessions; they make me feel guilty. You won't need me this weekend, will you?"

"Maybe. Why?"

"Because I won't be here," I explained. "I'll be out of town."

"How far out of town?"

"Palm Springs," I answered. "And I won't want to be bothered."

He frowned and then nodded. "All right. You and your

rich friends. Let me know when you're ready to hire some expensive help, Joe."

"I will. Good night, Sergeant. Good luck."

"Thanks to you," he said, "I've had it."

I went out and left him smiling, a new role for him. I turned the Plymouth west, heading for Mary's.

She should still be up.